Six Shamans and a Visionary

A Novella

Adriana Polito

Copyright © 2020 Adriana Polito

All rights reserved. ISBN: 9798638913618

DEDICATION

For my husband, Tom.
We could have spent quality time
together in the garden.
You encouraged me to start this book instead.
Thank you, my love.

I also dedicate this book to everyone around the
world who worked on the front line during the
Coronavirus Pandemic.

SIX SHAMANS AND A VISIONARY

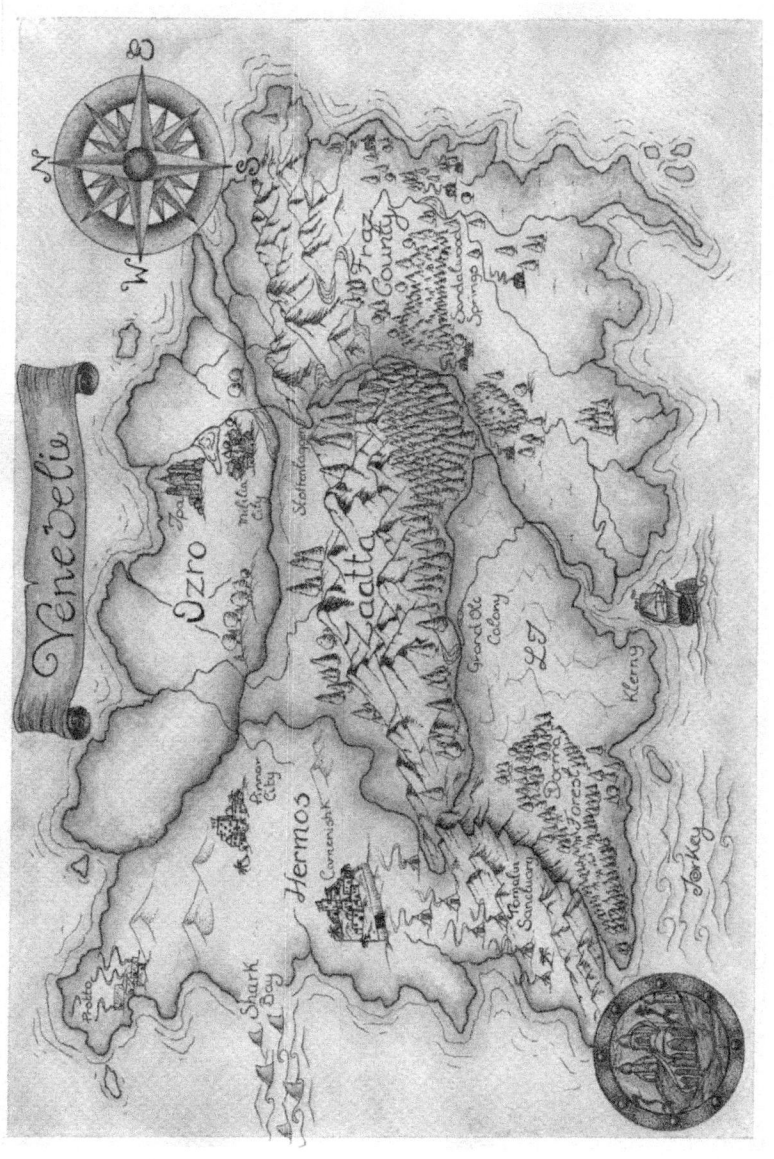

SIX SHAMANS AND A VISIONARY

SIX SHAMANS AND A VISIONARY

	Preface	
1	The night before the Pilgrimage on planet Venezeli	1
2	Laquó Mgamé	4
3	Shine Cedar	5
4	Colonius Bramblebush	7
5	Serenity Jupe	12
6	Carmen De La Luz	17
7	Luther Jung	23
8	Tremendos	26
9	From First Contact to the day before The Pilgrimage	30
10	The morning of The Pilgrimage	35
11	JUDGE 1: Tomms Day of Fraz County	41
12	JUDGE 2: Ignacius Prime of Ozro	47
13	JUDGE 3: Lara Trinkett of Ozro	55
14	JUDGE 4: Bird Night of Zaatta	66
15	JUDGE 5: Zoop Harvey of Zaatta	77

16	JUDGE 6: Shamus Montgomery of Hermos	83
17	JUDGE 7: Meradin Zykló of Hermos	87
18	JUDGE 8: Romins Perpula-Dawn of Hermos	97
19	JUDGE 9: Jakolyn Tempest of Li	104
20	JUDGE 10: Danny Dove of Li	117
21	JUDGE 11: Duandarin Krespos of planet Jenar	128
22	The Koli Ceremony	138

PREFACE

There is no villain in this story. Nobody dies. There's no inciting incident, no increase in tension, no climax or resolution. There's no formatted story arc – it just didn't happen that way.

This is a story about six Shamans and a Visionary, also known as 'The Collective'. It's about their year-long pilgrimage to find the founding Supreme Court Judges for planet Venezeli. There are eleven to find. Ten from Venezeli, and one from a neighbouring planet. And they find them all.

There are no major threats along the way. No dragons to fight or diseases to be afraid of. Put simply, this is a story about a group of healers, looking for people who hold certain characteristics. It isn't a literary masterpiece designed to woo you with stunning structure or prose. It's not interested in gripping your attention with three dimensional characters who like each other, then hate each other before making up in the last act. This story isn't about the reader - it's about the story, and what actually happened.

And here's what happened – a search for moral goodness. Not a quest or an epic adventure. A search followed by a discovery.

The people you're about to meet have emotions and personal motivating factors, of course they do.

But they've also been instructed to do a job and, put simply, they do it.

The people they're searching for are part of a collective destiny. These people have fears and reservations, but they find courage and accept the challenge.

This tale is about the personal interactions between those people. It's not about multiple, seemingly impossible-to-beat external dangers. It's not about enemies that are somehow defeated in the eleventh hour. These guys make it - nothing kills them along the way. This story is about a pilgrimage filled with hope. It's about the search for individuals with facets that make a well-rounded person and an extremely talented Supreme Court Judge.

These facets are Universal. They are love, compassion, virtue, loyalty, integrity, patience, wisdom and a balance of one's own duality. I might as well tell you now - the end isn't tied up in a big, satisfactory bow. It just ends. Twenty-eight years later, a new, more exciting story begins, but this one just ends. If you're still reading and want to know about this story, these people and why they were chosen, then please join us. If you don't, then that's ok. There are plenty of dramatic page-turners out there to make you laugh, cry and keep you continually on the edge of your seat. This just isn't one of them.

CHAPTER ONE
THE NIGHT BEFORE THE
PILGRIMAGE ON PLANET VENEZELI

Hispanica knew her mother was busy. She had 'that look.' It wasn't an unapproachable look, just one that filled her face. It filled it right up with busyness.

Hispanica was eight years old. She didn't know everything yet, but she knew when her mother was busy. She perched herself down on the window seat in the snug, looked out the window of their green wood- panelled house and straight up at the lunar sky. Fraz County had a dense pine and cedarwood fragrance in the air. You could smell it from every corner of this magical country. It hit you on the nose as soon as you crossed the border.

A Glup Jock was sitting on a branch in a nearby tree. Hispanica could never tell where those things were looking. Glup Jock's had no visible features on their ball-shaped fur body. They were round, with velvet triangle ears. This was the only thing that protruded from their round furry bodies. Hispanica knew this Glup Jock was either facing her or looking the other way. She rolled her tongue and trilled at it. It spun around on the spot. *It was looking at the lunar,* thought Hispanica. *Those things love looking at the lunar.*

Hispanica twirled a large section of her wavy golden- orange locks between her fingers. She decided to pluck up the courage and head into the study to interrupt her mother.

Cressida was hunched over a table filled with open books.

"Mother," Hispanica stepped into the study with curious timidity. Cressida seemed lost in a trance.

"Mother, what are you doing?"
Cressida turned around and looked at Hispanica. For a moment, Hispanica wasn't sure her mother recognised her.

"Mother, are you ok?"

"My darling! Come in, come all the way in little one."
Cressida gave her daughter a giant warm embrace. "Sorry about that my starlet. I was light years away."

"What are you doing? Is this for a coven meeting?"

"Oh, it's much more exciting than that my sweetheart."

Cressida sat herself down in a massive patchwork quilted chair. It was big enough to engulf both her and Hispanica, whom she has signaled to join her. Hispanica ran to her mother and snuggled into her lap.

"Six Shamans and a Visionary are going on a Pilgrimage tomorrow. They're going around our planet to find members of our new Supreme Court."

"Around the planet?"
Cressida nodded.

"Won't it take a while?"

"Yes, it will starlet. They have to find ten Judges here on Venezeli and then one from another planet."

"Who are these people?"

"We do not know, not yet. And they don't either. These are people who will come from all walks of life. Not lawyers or law makers as you might know them. They will be ordinary people with extraordinary abilities."

"Abilities? Like powers?"

"The best kind of superpowers there are – virtue, patience, balance, integrity, love, compassion and foresight."

"Who's going?"

"I have chosen our country's best Shamans for this job, and we have a Visionary. She's on her way now, from Li. She's arriving tonight."

"Do I know them?"

"Some of them, yes. You will have seen them around."

"Why have you chosen them, Mother?" Cressida kissed Hispanica on the forehead. "Settle in then starlet, and I'll tell you who and why…."

CHAPTER TWO
LAQUÓ MGAMÉ

"Laquó Mgamé was a banker before The Awakening. He loved numbers. Numbers where, to him, a language more beautiful than Constantine's poetry. He was born in Fraz County but moved to Ozro's administrative capital, Ipa, around five years before First Contact with Universe 4. He had six separate best suits, one for each day of work. Every Montag he would wash, dry and steam them ahead of the next working week. He loved method and logic. He didn't like crowds and preferred his own company. One day Laquó got ill. It made him re-evaluate everything. It made him really think about what was important to him. This was before The Awakening, before First Contact. So, you could say that Laquó Mgamé started his Shamanic journey well before the others. In fact, he was one of the first to offer his help to Lunar Roohama, Jimus Krakovia's right-hand woman. This was a man who had truly awoken, truly honed in on his strengths. He's still an unsociable hermit with a short temper, but he is virtuous, very virtuous. That is why I chose him, my little starlet. He will be able to recognise virtue, integrity and honour in others. And we need Judges like that. Someone who can take a good look at themselves and stand up for something bigger than themselves. Something that is for the greater good."

***

Laquó Mgamé was in his little woodcutter's hut at the edge of the forest. He was nervous about the next day's Pilgrimage. Would he have what it takes?

He went outside to chop some firewood. He looked up at the lunar and took a deep breath in. *Find the courage Laquó, you won't be alone.* Funnily enough, this was also the very thing that troubled him. He hadn't been around many people since The Awakening, only Jimus Krakovia's helpers and those who came to him for advice or guidance at his woodcutter's hut. He was not used to going out into the world. He'd shed his hunting instincts long ago, back with The Awakening.

Laquó Mgamé stepped back inside his hut and placed the logs on the fire. He went over to his sled bed to finish packing his bag. After this was done, he fixed himself a wheat whiskey and sat on the bed, staring at the fire. *Cressida must know what she's doing, doesn't she?*

CHAPTER THREE
SHINE CEDAR

"Shine Cedar was a dancer before The Awakening. Her transition from dancing to Shamanic witchery was a difficult one, but she persevered. A tragic accident had stopped her dancing altogether, but she discovered the power of healing and used it to nurse herself better.

The power of magic consumed her and she managed to fully heal and get back to dancing. Everyone thought it impossible, as did she for a long time, but her patience and perseverance got her there. To Shine's surprise, once she had achieved her goal of being able to dance again, she no longer loved it, well, not as much as she loved magic.

Shine had discovered something immensely powerful along the way. The impact of magic and the ways in which she could use it to help others, as a Shamanic witch. Shine set up her thatched cottage in the centre of Fraz County, near the cavern of Herratta, deep in the forest. She spent most of her days carefully crafting Lojo Dolls. These were tiny dolls made from fabric and straw which, once enchanted, could bring remote healing to people as far as Hermos, depending on your powers. But it was patience that was Shine's biggest attribute. Her journey of self-healing required a lot of courage. If you asked her, she wouldn't say so. Shine's thorn was one of a distinct lack of self-belief. She couldn't see how far she'd come and how much she had done for others. She just did what she could, a little at a time, day by day and hoped for the best. But what Shine didn't realise, and possibly still doesn't, is that it's her attention to detail and patience that creates a thousand tiny ripples. These ripples accumulate and do you know what they turn into my darling? They turn into a great big wave."

***

Shine was making her tenth Lojo Doll of the evening. Her cottage was full of gas lights, each one a little different. Some were warm yellow, others green and blue. Some shone brightly, others dimly.

As Shine sat at her workshop desk, something hit off her windowpane, sending a cracking sound through the cottage. Shine jumped, startled, almost pricking her finger. She put down her Lojo Doll and went outside to have a look. The front garden was bathed in lunarlight. Shine's lavender and Gojine bedding plants looked like a plush purple quilt in this light. She looked under her windowpane and found a medium-sized stone with a white ribbon around it. The ribbon hugged a piece of paper to the stone's surface. Shine carefully untied the ribbon, had a look out into the woods, then looked down at the paper. It was a handwritten note. It said:

*Good luck tomorrow Shine. I love you,
always have, always will.*

And that was it - no name attached.

It mattered not. It was exactly what Shine had needed in that moment. She folded the note delicately and put it inside the pendulum locket around her neck.

CHAPTER FOUR
COLONIUS BRAMBLEBUSH

"Colonius Bramblebush was an antique dealer before The Awakening. He's always had a good eye for seeing the value in things, but that's not his gift starlet. His gift is that of impartiality. To see things with a clear perspective and still be able to maintain a distance from your own thoughts and feelings. It's quite a skill, and Colonius Bramblebush is very good at this. Tomorrow he is on his way, with five other Shamans and a Visionary, to choose some of the most crucial decision makers we will have on our planet, our very own Guardians of morals and ethics."

***

As a little boy, Colonius was often judged and put under enormous pressure by his wealthy socialite parents. It was a burden that Colonius carried around for most of his life. He knew exactly how it felt to feel undervalued, to feel like you were never good enough. He'd had enough of the fake parties his parents held every month. He'd had enough of their private school expectations.

When Colonius was seventeen years old, he packed a bag and left his townhouse on the outskirts of Ozro's Metrolopitan District, Ipa, and headed straight to the administrative capital. Colonius became an antique dealer and traded mostly in the Grassmarket area. Colonius witnessed a lot of shady comings and goings. He never felt like he was in the right life. He made a lot of zulan from his time in Ipa, but contentment still didn't come. At age twenty-two, Colonius headed to Zaatta and spent five years working alongside the Zaattan monks, helping them with community projects and archaeological digs.

The Zaattan monks are some of the most balanced individuals in all of Venezeli. They had been going long before The Awakening. Colonius learnt a lot about Zaattan's rich geological history, and his ability for balance and impartial perspective improved with every year he spent with the monks. Something that did not go away entirely was a deep-seated sense of pride and a slight arrogance. Colonius Bramblebush could see things clearly alright, but there was still a part of him, that little boy, who was scared. When Colonius felt threatened or afraid, that little boy would come out and try to get the upper hand. He always realised the origin of his actions after the fact, so apt were his observational skills. He knew it came from a deep-seated issue with his overbearing and snooty parents, something he had not yet properly addressed - with them or himself.

Colonius was twenty-seven years old when The Awakening happened. He had sensed a shift but wasn't sure what was coming. Three weeks after it, Colonius moved to Fraz County to become an amulet hunter. He set up his own collection of amulets. Amulets are charms that are incredibly special to Shamans; they are blessed with good luck for big journeys, in this life or the next.

Colonius opened his research museum in the main village in Fraz County, Sandalwood Springs. Many Shamans would come to him for amulets. Colonius would go in search for them in all corners of Venezeli. It was in this museum that he first met Cressida. Cressida saw something in him straight away. A very decent and true quality – she could tell he was a good man. Cressida and Colonius became friends and after a while she enticed him over to the Shamanic teachings. That was eight years ago.

He was a significant help with the Prophetic Journals. Colonius suggested the best resting place for them, which is where they will go just before the Koli Ceremony in Ipa. The Shamans and Visionary will have a separate ceremony just for the Journals in Fraz County. The Journals will lie somewhere deep in the Herratta cavern for all the years to come, until Universe 5 makes First Contact of its own.

Colonius Bramblebush looked down the lens of an antique Hermosian guanta rifle. His target was an old tin can on his garden wall, illuminated by the night's pooling lunarlight. He took a steady breath in. On his exhale he paused, then pulled the trigger at the end of his exhaling breath. The tin can flew into the air then jetted off to the left-hand side, like it changed its mind last minute and wanted to go left instead of up. Colonius put down the rifle and smiled. He was ready for the Pilgrimage tomorrow. He felt born ready for this. What would his parents think of this? They didn't even know that he'd been practicing Shamanism for the last eight years, they thought he still searched for and sold amulets. *Never mind what they think. This is about the greater good, the leaders of our tomorrow.*

It bugged Colonius that he still craved his parents' acceptance and approval. He was forty-three years old, why did this still matter to him? Colonius picked up his rifle and the empty cans and walked back into his cabin-come-Shaman-hut-come-museum. Colonius liked being close to his collection. Despite The Awakening and his change in profession, Colonius Bramblebush still had an enormous collection of amulets and other archaeological treasures from over the years. He'd had a few theft attempts on his collection recently, which was surprising. The Awakening had significantly decreased that kind of negative behaviour.

Everyone had been on a much more cooperative path since The Awakening. It was like a new understanding of the fragility of our lives, and it put a lot of things into perspective. These were things which Colonius already had plenty of perspective on, but the early years of The Awakening were a welcomed change in Colonius' view. We had a shared experience, a shared sense of survival. Gone was the desire to fight one another. A greater uniting purpose had been revealed. It brought out the best in everyone in Universe 5 - except for the citizens of planet Trumponia. They failed exceptionally.

Trumponians didn't change before, during or after The Awakening. No-one could understand why they still couldn't work well together, but Colonius knew. He knew that Trumponians were greedy narcissists. They were more interested in self-advancement and commercial gain than they were about working together for the well-being of their fellow citizens. And so, after many reckless decisions, a lot of inaction and unnecessary risks, Trumponians completely obliterated Trumponia and everyone in it. There's always one idiotic planet - all galaxies and Universes have them. For now,

Colonius was excited about Venezeli's chances as one of the competing planets. He had a feeling in his gut that it would be a Venezelian to make First Contact with the next Universe out there, whenever and with whomever that would be.

CHAPTER FIVE
SERENITY JUPE

"Serenity Jupe is one of the most 'at one' individuals I have ever met. Sure, by looking at her you would think she worships the dark side of the scale, and you wouldn't be wrong. But she also worships the good side, and that's what makes her perfectly balanced. Sometimes her humour or playfulness is lost on people. She can come across a bit potty-mouthed. She has been accused of having a dark sense of humour and might be quite scary to the judging eye, however, I have never met a more integrated individual. It is entirely because of Serenity's assimilation of her dark side, that she is not only its friend, but its master. It doesn't control her, directly or indirectly. She is always aware of its presence, and therefore it can never take her by surprise. Her Shadow is always at the party, with plenty of snacks and just as much attention as it needs. No more, no less. In fact, Serenity understood it was often those who paraded under the guise of good that were most evil in their actions. They were individuals who didn't acknowledge their dark side at all and were thus puppets of it. Or they were those who frequented with it a little too much and had completely lost hold of the rope that had been attaching them to the shore.

Serenity was born in Hermos, in a Tomalin Sanctuary. Her mother was a nurse, and her father was a vetenary nurse. Serenity's father was obsessed with Tomalins: small, delightful creatures that looked like a cross between an Earth Chinese Pika and a South American Olinguito. In other words, perfectly cute, just like you, my beautiful Hispanica. Serenity grew up in the Sanctuary alongside the Tomalins. She learned all about their habits, skills and nature, as well as how to communicate with them. Serenity's mother cared for the Venezelian families in the Sanctuary. There were around ten families living there when Serenity was young, and their main purpose was to study and care for the Tomalins. Tomalins were on the brink of extinction when Serenity's family moved there. Serenity's mother was around six months pregnant at the time. Serenity was around Tomalins from before she was born. Tomalins cannot speak, but they do have an incredible sense of humour. They are fiercely protective of their fellow Venezelians and of each other. They have huge hearts that are filled with love and compassion. Unfortunately, when some of Universe 5's planets developed the technology to travel through space and physically visit their neighbouring planets, it brought with it a lot of unwanted tourism. Indigans had a fascination for Hermos on planet Venezeli. Its desert landscapes were a favourite holiday destination for Indigans. Indigans lived on a planet that was mostly volcanic and hilly. It had one continent, like Venezeli, but it was a lot smaller. The flat desert plane and furry brown and white Tomalins were of great interest to the Indigans. Unfortunately, over time, planet Indigo developed a band of entrepreneurial pirates who loved to bargain. They were intimidating, but valued deals and bartering over violence. These Indigan pirates started to steal Tomalins from their environment, taking them back to Indigo to work as slaves on the Indigan volcanic hills, collecting things like Herenaga fruit and vegetables. Their small hands, bodies and stamina levels meant that they were perfect for that type of work - according to Indigan businesspeople. Once news spread of this, people from all over Venezeli came to the Hermosian Outback and helped build a barrier around the Tomalin Sanctuary. Eventually, the pirates backed off. After The Awakening, the pirates had a whole new game to occupy them. The Tomalins felt safe again. Serenity grew up in the Sanctuary. She worked alongside her mother and father, taking care of the community and the Tomalins. One day Colonius Bramblebush was on an expedition for amulets in the Hermosian desert. He saw Serenity at the edge of The Sanctuary. She was bandaging a Tomalin's wrist. He wasn't sure how or why, but he knew she had something special about her. He went to speak with her and of course, she had no idea what he was talking about. She knew about the rise of the Shamanic movement, but it would take a lot for her to leave her family and the Tomalins. When The Awakening happened, she remembered Colonius' visit. Being good at reading signs, she packed her bags, said goodbye to her family and friends and moved out to Fraz County around a week later. That was thirteen years ago. Colonius had recruited a Shaman before becoming one himself! But he couldn't have been more right. Serenity runs a practice in the village, and she specializes in duality studies. She runs classes every week, and when you're a bit older, you can go and check them out if you like."

***

Serenity loved the colour black. She was always dressed in it. The people of Fraz County were a very colourful people, often draped in long, soft hessian gowns of a million colours. Serenity was different. Black made her heart feel light. Black made her mood feel uplifted. Melancholy songs excited her. Serenity didn't revel in sadness or misfortune - far from it. Her closeness to the dark and macabre made her feel strong - she felt like she understood all of life's angles. She didn't feel like a master of life. She just tried her best to navigate herself, and others, through it the best she could.

Serenity saw life as a body of water. The Roko Sea engulfs just one continent in Venezeli - the Roko continental plate. This large, singular piece of land mass holds all Venezeli's countries. As one continent, this means that the countries all share borders as well as a singular, continuous coastline. The countries in Venezeli are Ozro, Zaatta, Fraz County, Li and Hermos. All parts are important. Just as all parts of the Universe are important. With wholeness come parts. With parts, come opposites, or duality patterns. Serenity knew this from an incredibly early age.

Tonight, she was sat on the steps outside her little Shamanic practice. She had a book upturned on her lap and a hot cup of gingero tea in her hands. She took a sip and enjoyed the warm and soothing sensation as it went down her throat. The street was empty. She could hear the faint sound of the nearby springs that gave the village its name. The springs made a whistling sound as they meandered through the heart of the village. *So alive.*

SIX SHAMANS AND A VISIONARY

Serenity saw life as a body of water. It was something so powerful that it was impossible to overpower it - but it was possible to learn how to harmonise with it. She felt it was important to learn how to show it respect. How to ask it for mercy. How to remind it that you knew how powerful it was, and how powerful it could be. It could raise you up over the waves and make you feel alive, more alive than you have ever felt. In the same heartbeat, it could crash you into the surf, and plummet you into its deep dark watery arms. Ignoring the seas' potential never turned out well. Ignoring its messages was ill-advised. Understanding its meaning and honouring its potential was always the wisest move. Serenity stood up and took a long look at the heart of Sandalwood Springs. She knew The Collective would find those eleven individuals. They would protect the whole. *Good things are coming, all good things.*

CHAPTER SIX
CARMEN DE LA LUZ

"Carmen De La Luz is the embodiment of truest and purest love. The Collective wouldn't be complete without her skills. Carmen will be able to see right into the heart of you – she sees all the goodness first. Carmen was born in Li. Her father was an artist and her mother used to work in the fisheries. She grew up on the beaches of Klerny, a small fishing and mining town. Carmen liked to go to Klerny harbour with her father. They would paint the boats, the birds and the fisher people. At night, she would help her mother prepare the fish for the trading posts. Both Carmen's parents applied a very gentle, diligent and respectful touch to their professions. They honoured the canvas, and they honoured the sacrificial killing of the fish. Carmen knew about the circle of life, but the thing she felt the most, was love."

***

Carmen had always felt close to her mother and father. Her mother could be frosty with strangers, but once she got to know them, she would treat them like family Carmen's father used to travel with his artwork. He'd hold exhibitions all over Venezeli. Most of his artwork was inspired by the sea. He was always around strangers. Sometimes he trusted them too much and was naïve of their intentions. Carmen knew she was loved dearly by them both. It was this knowledge that gave her a certain confidence in life.

Carmen loved nature. She used to spend a lot of time around the quarry, watching the workers dig for granite. Li was renowned for its granite. Another thing Li was renowned for was its music. She would often follow the workers home through the forest, keeping her distance behind them. A lady would start to sing. A man would play the Killerno, a small guitar that makes the most beautiful sounds you could ever imagine. Soon, the forest was filled with song, voices eerily travelling through the tree branches. As Carmen walked barefoot through the tall grass in the forest, listening to the workers after a long day at the quarry, she felt her heart might burst. Carmen's heart felt everything.

One late afternoon she went down to the fisheries to see if she could help her mother. As she arrived at the harbour, she caught sight of a Snooper bird descending towards the water for a fish. As it swooped, the suruplight's rays bounced off the water and hit the Snooper's feathers with a crystal brilliance. It took Carmen's breath away. A Desert Shark approached. It had lost its way and ended up in Li waters, far from Hermos' seas. Carmen watched as its fin sparkled in the evelight. The Snooper bird saw it approach and retreated to the clouds. It was approaching midlight. *What a world we live in*, she thought.

Carmen didn't always make the right decisions in life, but she tried to lead from the heart. Sometimes Carmen got herself into bad situations, she was a little naïve at times. She trusted too much, loved too much and struggled to see the more negative underlying motivations in people.

***

"Why did you choose Carmen, mother?"

"Carmen is special, my little one. This is why I chose her to join The Collective. They need someone who will be able to see into a person's soul, their inner drum, their fundamental moral compass. To see if they feel anything towards others, and whether those feelings have others' best interests at heart. She will be a good addition to the team... How did she become a Shaman? That's a good question sweetheart, but, you see, see was always a Shaman - she was born one. Carmen didn't know this until she came here, but her grandparents, on both her mother and father's side, came from a long line of witches. Carmen's parents didn't harness those skills in their lifetime, but Carmen became aware of her ability to help people and heal at quite an early age. She came to Fraz County around four years ago. She hasn't been practising as long as the others in the coven, but she has an insight that is very rare to find."

***

Night Before The Pilgrimage

Carmen was out of breath by the time she reached her tent by the sea. She'd run all the way back from the deep forest plane. She was happy that the lunar was still high and shimmering on the calm waters over the mid Fraz County coast. The waters in Li were far choppier. This was because it was an industrious country, a busy and bustling merchant trading area. She had never known a single bustling or stressed-out individual from all her time here in Fraz County. People who came here tended to mellow out very quickly, even if they weren't that way inclined.

Carmen took off her sandals and sat on a blanket outside her tent. She picked up a handful of stones from the sand. She loved the feeling of sand through her fingers, soft and reliable. She rustled the stones in her right hand so that the sand sprinkled out between her fingers and the stones made a clackety-clack sound. Carmen closed her eyes. She could hear a forest moose in the woods behind her. The stones in her hand were still rustling and she could hear the small waves ahead of her, webbing back and forth on the beach. Carmen delighted in the sandwich of sounds under the night sky. There was another sound in her ear – it was her heartbeat.

Carmen was excited about the Pilgrimage. She was filled with hope and honoured that Cressida had picked her to join The Collective. That night, Carmen's heart was beating extra hard. She pulled some white ribbon from her left pocket and held it tight in her hand, as if it was the most precious thing in the world to her. But it wasn't the ribbon that was precious - it was Shine Cedar.

It had always been Shine Cedar, from the first moment she saw her. Carmen had just arrived in Sandalwood Springs with nothing more than a rucksack, a tent and her favourite sandals. Four years on, and she hadn't acquired much more in the way of possessions, but Carmen never felt a need for possessions. She had a book of her father's drawings and paintings and two of her mother's handkerchiefs. The handkerchiefs always stayed on her person. Carmen knew that one day, she would give one of those handkerchiefs to her beloved on their wedding day. The other would continue to travel with her, always. These were the most valuable possessions she owned.

When Carmen first arrived in Sandalwood Springs, she found a bench to sit on and pulled out a map. She was looking for Cressida's wooden house. She knew it was in Banks Elms forest but didn't know which direction to go once there. It was at this point that Shine Cedar swooped by on her bicycle. Shine saw Carmen on the bench and stopped to say hello. Shine asked if Carmen needed any help. And that was it. That was the moment that Carmen De La Luz fell in love with Shine Cedar. Shine had accompanied her to Cressida's house that afternoon. Along the way, they talked about the latest fleet of dreamers who were going to pass on information to the other planets in the boundary zone. They talked about the Prophetic Journals. They talked about the massive task ahead for the Shamans as they continued to copy the original text from Jimus Krakovia's records. In fact, this was the reason that Carmen had come to Fraz County. She wanted to help the Shamans in the transcription process.

After a week at Cressida's, the Shaman leader knew that there was much more planned for Carmen than just transcribing. She had a talent that could not be wasted. Cressida fast-tracked Carmen in the Shamanic teachings and introduced her to the community. It wasn't a hard transition; Carmen had it in her blood. Should Venezeli be involved in the next multi-dimensional Universal race to make First Contact, Cressida knew that Carmen would be of pivotal importance. Carmen had a way of turning up for things at just the right time. She had always struggled to turn up for her own love story at the right time, but she was working on that.

Carmen and Shine became best friends. Shine taught her Shamanic rituals and how to make Lojo Dolls. They were inseparable. When Carmen discovered that they had both been chosen for The Collective, her heart almost exploded. This was it. This was the moment that Carmen could be brave. She would tell Shine how she felt. The Pilgrimage was due to last a year, more or less. She hoped that would be enough time to pluck up the courage and tell Shine that it was her who wrote the note.

CHAPTER SEVEN
LUTHER JUNG

"Luther Jung is my favourite. I know I'm not supposed to have favourites starlet, but, sometimes, a favourite shines through, and mine is Luther. Luther was born Luther Marcus Kresley Grimley Jung. You have met him many times, so I don't need to tell you how charming he is. But it is not his charm that got my attention – it is his compassion for others. Luther Jung understands the Venezelian condition more than anyone I've ever met. And not just for Venezelians, any life force or species. This is a man who would put his life on the line for a stranger. He believes that injustice anywhere is injustice everywhere. He is true and virtuous and selfless beyond measure. But he is also stubborn and determined and ever so slightly proud. He does not like to fail, he is fiercely loyal and protective of the ones he loves, but he can also be very stubborn. Did I already mention that he could be stubborn? As with all beings, we have strengths and weaknesses and sometimes these characteristics can spin back on themselves, depending on the situation at hand. Many a time, Luther's extreme focus, passion and determination has resulted in life-changing positivity for many people. Other times it has caused conflict and danger. Sometimes his compassion has saved lives, in ways he cannot comprehend, such as a listening ear, an encouraging embrace or an offer of help. Other times, his complete commitment to others means that he sometimes overlooked himself and his own health and wellbeing. Luther may not be the most balanced of Shamans, but he has a fire that burns bright. It is this fire that ignites hope and justice for many. And justice is what we are looking for. I have every faith that Luther will be instrumental in finding us some fantastic Judges for the Supreme Court. Yes, he is also very handsome darling, that's right. But that's not why he's mother's favourite. Honestly, it isn't!"

***

Luther Jung was taking a bath in his modest little wooden hut at the edge of the Banks Elms forest. The hut had four rooms: a kitchen, where Luther's bath stood; a study, which was also his Shamanic practice; a small living space, which was also his dining room and a bedroom.

Luther was born in Fraz County. His father was a preacher, and his mother was a teacher from Ozro. His parents had met at a conference in Ipa and soon, Madelina Bravos was Mrs. Henry Jung. She moved to Fraz County and set up home with Henry. Luther was now living in what was their original family home. His parents were now in a hillside cabin with views of the beach. They lived a simple and happy life, and Luther, an only child, dedicated his life to them and his community.

Luther had started off life as a teacher, teaching in the local Sandalwood Springs elementary school. He had his heart broken by one Leeying Crown. Leeying came to teach at the school for one semester before moving to Ozro to work in a private school. Luther was crushed. He had just started his

Shamanic teachings and his mother had fallen ill. Leeying knew that he could not leave Fraz County at this time. He didn't want to stop her from following her dream either, of one day becoming an education consultant for the Administrative Capital in Ipa, so he let her go. Luther was never the same after that. He intensified his focus on social justice issues. He was pioneering them well before The Awakening. After it, he turned his attention to Shamanism, hoping that he could be of some use to the cause. As a resident of Fraz County, Luther was already aware of the growing Shamanic community there, and it didn't take long before he was a big part of it.

Luther stepped out of his bath and dried himself off. He looked out of his window. The lunarlight was capping the forest with bright silver glow. Luther knew he was ready for this Pilgrimage. He would do his best for Cressida and the cause. He hoped that after the Pilgrimage there would be plenty to do. He was keen to help, and wanted to keep his mind off Leeying, who had just announced her engagement to an investment banker in Ipa.

CHAPTER EIGHT
TREMENDOS

"Tremendos is a beautiful creature, just wait until you see her starlet! She looks like a beautiful mermaid, but with legs. Tremendos is a Visionary, she's the one coming from Li. She has long hair and high cheekbones. Her eyes have a liquid metallic swirl to them, like pools of blue and green sparkling ink pots. Visionaries tend to wear long, flowing grey robes, they all do this. Visionaries have been around for a long time - well before The Awakening. They can live anywhere, but most Visionaries come from a settlement in Li. Many are born there or travel there to harness their skills. After The Awakening, there was a huge surge of new talent, as with all souls trying to find their true calling. Tremendos was part of a lengthy line of ancient Visionaries.

She gets particularly excited about a man she calls 'Leonardo Da Vinci.' No one knows who this man is or what planet he's from. Funnily enough, neither does Tremendos. This is just a glimpse she has had from either the past or the future. She doesn't know where he's from, or if he is past or future, but she's a great fan of his work. After The Awakening, she tried searching for him in our Universe through dream travel but hasn't had any success. She suspects he could from a different

Universe, possibly one we haven't even discovered yet.

Cool things to know about Tremendos: she can get energy from enchanted amulets; she can see glimpses of past and future events by touching objects or people and, she can understand and talk to plants and animals.

Tremendos is the queen of foresight in this group. The Collective will benefit from her skills as they venture out onto this Pilgrimage. She will also be a key player in identifying good potential Judges. She is loyal beyond compare. Like most Visionaries, she can be distant. This is not intentional behaviour. It's just that their mind is often preoccupied with signs, symbols and visions, so they aren't always able to engage with others around them in the more traditional ways. Many Visionaries also have difficulty in showing emotions. This is not because they don't feel emotion, it's just that their interpretation of emotion is processed differently. It's important to understand that whilst some of the Shamans are guided by instinct and feelings, Visionaries are guided by information, and the ability to process that information very quickly and efficiently. Visionaries are incredibly loyal to their family and friends. They can show enormous bravery and courage. They go into an extremely strict ritualistic training programme from an early age to develop their skills. They spend up to ten hours a day studying and practising. Tremendos was a top student at her settlement in the Droma Forest, and now she teaches there. Tomorrow she will be joining The Collective on the Pilgrimage, and they will be most happy and grateful to have her."

***

SIX SHAMANS AND A VISIONARY

Tremendos was in a horse-drawn carriage currently heading East into Fraz County. She'd left earlier in the afternoon and would arrive at the Inn in Sandalwood Springs just after midnight. As the horse hooves made a clickety-clack sound on the country road through the back forests of Li, Tremendos closed her eyes and descended into what she called her 'blank zone.' It was a sanctuary, a void where Tremendos could temporarily shut off her mind to any incoming messages or visions. They were heading North East and inland, away from the Li coastline, however Tremendos could still smell the salty sea air. Her carriage window was open and lunarlight was tickling her eyelids. She went deeper into her blank zone. She heard music, it sounded like a Killerno, but she knew it wasn't outside the carriage. It was coming from her memories. In front of her eyes she saw nothing, nothing but a blanket of aqua marine-coloured waves. It looked like a colourful bedsheet, distended on a washing line. It moved gently in front of her, she felt calmed and relaxed by it.

Suddenly, the sheet fell from the imaginary washing line. Tremendos' vision was clear – she saw a hunket-clench banging down on a metallic surface. The metal-on-metal sound was excruciating. It certainly caught her attention. The hunket-clench disintegrated like a reflection in a pool of water. The body of water increased into a massive wave. Bright suruplight shone out of the wave in every direction. Fish and Snooper birds swirled all around it. The smell of the sea was even stronger now. She saw a limitless sea horizon ahead of her. Tremendos opened her eyes. The visions evaporated. *Well, that was interesting.* Tremendos noted the images down in her small golden notebook, as she always did. She hoped that at some point the visions would make contextual sense in her reality. Tremendos looked out the window and smiled. She was honoured to be part of The Collective. She had the usual anxieties about being around other people, but she had always got on well with Shamans. She hoped that they would do some excellent work together.

CHAPTER NINE
FROM FIRST CONTACT TO
THE DAY BEFORE THE PILGRIMAGE

It had been sixteen years since Jimus Krakovia made First Contact with Sister Pretya. It seemed fitting that The Collective should start their Pilgrimage tomorrow. Jimus Krakovia's address to the citizens of planet Freyal had sparked The Awakening. People were catapulted into harnessing their skills. They started to seek out their true calling. From the day of his address, Jimus Krakovia spent the next five years transcribing the secrets of the Universe. These had been passed on by Sister Pretya, from her mind, to his. From here, Jimus was responsible for re-directing the information from his mind, directly into the Prophetic Journals.

After this came the Communication Years. Freyal citizens were taught how to dream travel. They were enlisted to spread the word to their neighbouring planets. A domino effect ensued. It would take eleven years for Jimus Krakovia's primary instructions to travel between galaxies and across Universe 5. And those primary instructions were clear - one day, in the near or distant future, Universe 5 would make contact with another, unknown Universe. They would either grind past each other (transform), collide with each other (converge) or glide over / under each other (subduction).

There were now five awoken Universes out there. The Journals stated that there were others - the unawake. These were the ones that you wanted to connect with.

Once this happened, gravitational boundary zones would make themselves known. This was the part of one Universe that was touching another. Any life-bearing galaxies within the boundary zones would have to mobilize a new way of living. This included a new justice system, a new society and a new purpose. The art of competition would once again take its place. The game was simple too - to be the first planet in the boundary zone to make First Contact with another living being in that neighbouring Universe.

Everyone would be able to see and stay updated on the competing planets' developments. A Universal contest would arise, keeping the Cosmos thoroughly entertained in the process.

The Bromidine galaxy existed within Universe 5, the fifth Universe to be discovered and the next in line to do the reaching out. Through a mixture of chance and geographical tectonic plate movement, the same section of Universe 5 that had been infiltrated by Universe 4 (via their contact, Sister Pretya), glided its way South on the Spherical Ball Of Life.

Fifteen years after Krakovia's address, the South- Eastern edge of Universe 5 started to glide over the North-Western edge of Universe 6. As soon as the eligible competing planets and reachable planets were identified, the game had begun. That was a year ago.

Since The Awakening itself, a community of Shamanic witches started to rise from the ashes. This happened organically in planets and galaxies all over Universe 5. These were healers who had faced dark times and come through the other side. They didn't know it yet, but Jimus Krakovia had a unique directive for Shamans living in the identified boundary zones and competing planets. They would become facilitators of the Prophecy itself - gatekeepers of the Universe's most secret hidden messages. Only these Shamans would have direct access to the Prophetic Journals, scribed by Jimus Krakovia himself. Krakovia was to choose a leader from each Shamanic community on each competing planet. These leaders would act as main council to their covens. Their life's work would become the copying of Journals, the protection of its contents and enlistment of a coven good enough to see the signs.

There was a lot to do on the operational front too. The Construction Years started after The Communication Years. In fact, The Construction Years could only begin once Universal contact had been made. What followed was a galaxy-wide drive to get the competing planets up and running.

This was year one of the Construction Years. It was anticipated that it would take a further four to five years to complete all the structures and systems required for the completing planets' new societies.

Multi Existential Windows had to be created. These were sophisticated scientific research centres, designed to analyse dreamer data. They were also tasked with identifying anyone who showed promise. This meant any dreamer who gave the impression that they could see beyond their own dimensionality. On Venezeli, this science centre went by the name MEW5. Its main directive was to deploy dream travellers to Universe 6 and then study their feedback.

Another area of construction for the competing planets are the governing bodies – CERNs. This stands for Consciousness Evolution Review Nest. Its purpose is to monitor MEW5s work (for its planet only), record any inter-galactic communication with Universe 6, and to take care of home affairs (for operational and administrative departments).

An academy or training school for dream travellers was in development too. The school's main purpose was to harness the planets' best travellers. It was looking for dream travellers with an aptitude for going long distances and gathering accurate information.

Last, but not least, was the creation of the Supreme Courts. The Supreme Court building was already under construction, but it was years away from completion. Jimus Krakovia had ordered the Shamanic leaders from each competing planet to choose their Collectives. Collectives were to be prepared for the Pilgrimage. Their main objective was to choose future Judges, Judges who would have the highest form of power in the competing planets.

Our story focuses on Planet Venezeli's Collective. It focuses on this planet because, unbeknown to anyone, not even Jimus Krakovia, this would be the planet that makes First Contact with Universe 6 - twenty-eight years from now.

The Prophetic Journals have signs, symbols and clues. They hold bits and pieces of guidance and advice. No one, at this point, knew that it would be one Marcux Grentil of Ozro, Venezeli who would be the one to make First Contact with Aurora Black of the United Kingdom, Earth. But how could they know this? Neither Marcux nor Aurora were born yet.

CHAPTER TEN
THE MORNING OF THE PILGRIMAGE

The Collective had gathered at Cressida's green wood- panelled house in Banks Elms forest. Luther had made up two massive pots of hot drinks on the stove, one with kaffee and the other gingero tea. The group were sitting in Cressida's kitchen, wherever they could grab a seat.

"Good morning everyone. Some of you might have expected a more glamorous send off from the village hall, something officious and grand," Cressida says smiling, knowing full well that the Shamans would never have expected such a thing. "yet here we are in my humble kitchen – welcome, my humble coven."

Colonius starts off a round of applause, the others join in. Cressida smiles and waves them to stop.

"This is a story about Six Shamans and a Visionary. This is your part of the story. I know that none of you underestimate the importance of what you are about to embark on. I know that you all fully understand what you're about to do, and how it will shape this planet's future. That is why you are sitting here. Jimus Krakovia trusted me to choose you, and I trust you to choose them. That's all we have – trust and hope. But that's enough, it's all we need to get through this. Take care of each other, I know you will. Challenge each other. If someone has a deep instinct telling them someone's choice might be wrong, voice that. Voice it the way we always voice our concerns in coven meetings. This is the longest amount of time that you will probably ever spend with each other. Make the most of it. Learn from each other, grow from each other, and, above all, look after yourselves and each other. You know what to do."

Hispanica appears in the kitchen doorway.

"Come in, starlet!"

Hispanica makes her way into the room. Members of The Collective pat her head and give her hugs as she makes her way past them and up to her mother.

"Hispanica has something that she'd like to give you. We have some good luck amulets for you and for your future Judges. Take two each for now. Someone can take the remaining four."

Hispanica picks up a basket containing eighteen charmed amulets. They are flat jade stones, in the shape of an inward circular fern frond.

"It means new beginnings, new life." says Hispanica as she hands Luther two amulets from the basket. Luther smiles at her. He puts the spare amulet in his breast pocket, then takes his one, kisses it and puts it in his jacket pocket. "I'll take the extra four, if you like?"

Hispanica hesitates, then remembers that someone would have to carry the extra amulets.

"Don't worry starlet, I'll keep them safe."

Hispanica smiles and grabs four more amulets for Luther.

"Please keep yourself safe too - you're my mother's favourite." Luther laughs at this and ruffles Hispanica's curly hair.

The Collective set off, leaving Banks Elms forest on the outskirts of Sandalwood Springs. They headed forty-five miles North, towards Trinkett's Clearing; a wood enclosed campsite in a hilly section of North Fraz County. The group started to unpack their overnight camping gear. Luther set up the campfire and cooking area. Laquó collected some logs to sit on, whilst Serenity and Colonius collected wood for burning.

Serenity dusted some leaves off the back of Colonius' robe.

"So, C, who do you think is going to bag the most Judges then? Fancy a wager?"

Colonius smiled. He knew his friend's competitive and playful nature only too well.

"A barrel of fire-cracker wheat whiskey says I find more than you." Colonius said as he packed some thin twigs for kindling into his side rucksack.

Serenity laughed a hearty chuckle. Colonius loved the wrinkles that accumulated around her eyes and cheeks when she laughed. She had a mischievous twinkle in her eyes which he found adorable.

"You are on my friend! One full barrel of wheat whiskey!"

"Fire-cracker wheat whiskey, not regular wheat whiskey."

"Not a problem, I like the fiery stuff."

"I know," said Colonius, "and so do the staff at Christian's Bar."

Serenity threw a pinecone at her friend. "Hey there, I'm not in there *that* much."

"It's practically your second home! I always call there before calling your place. I know that Christian is pleased about your custom, he has no issue with that, not at all." Colonius teased.

Serenity blushed, and quickly changed the subject.

"Have we got enough wood yet?"

***

The Collective were sitting around the thriving campfire as they finished off their apfel bars. The surup had set thirty minutes ago and Colonius had grabbed a bundle of blankets and distributed them across the group. Laquó thanked Colonius but waivered his blanket.

"I think we ought to change our itinerary for tomorrow."

Luther replied. "And why is that?"

"Well, we're about to head deep into Charno Territory and they have no idea we're coming."

"There are rumours going around about this Pilgrimage, people will know we're due to visit."

"Yes, that's true, Luther, but they don't know it's us."

"Should it matter?"

Laquó didn't like Luther's tone. It was clear to the others that Laquó and Luther were engaging in a battle for the Alpha role. It was a tension that had been there for years.

"No," replied Laquó, "our anonymity is a helpful thing, but you know what some Charnos are like. They've been relatively untouched by The Awakening."

"Be that as it may, we still have a duty to go there. The next Judge of the Supreme Court could be there. You never voiced this in our coven meetings. Why are you bringing this up now?"

"I don't know, a change in the air."

"You're not getting cold feet about the North Country, are you Laquó?" asked Serenity.

"Of course not. I don't know, it's just a feeling."

Tremendos was watching Laquó closely. She sensed fear in his face, a fear no-one else could see.

Carmen saw Shine rummage about in her bag. "What you looking for?"

"I brought some Lojo Dolls. I thought I could do a safety enchantment on them, pass them out to the group."

"That's nice."

"Who do you think will be first?"

"To find a Judge?" asked Carmen. Shine nods.

"Hard to say. It could be months from now, it could be weeks. We just need to stay alert and do our best." Carmen watched as Shine gently lay the dolls out on the pine-needled earth in front of her.

"How are you feeling about this journey?"

"Ok. I feel ok."

"We'll be fine. But I still like the idea of those safety Lojo Dolls." Carmen stands up. "I'm just going to say hello to Tremendos, see if she's settling in."

Tremendos was on the other side of the campfire, her eyes were still fixated on Laquó. Carmen thought that she was having a vision. She shuffled onto the log next to her, approaching gently so as not to startle her. "Hi."

Tremendos wasn't startled at all, it was hard to startle her.

"Hello."

"Would you like a blanket?"

"I'm alright thank you."

"I wasn't disturbing you, was I? You know, up there." asked Carmen.

Tremendos laughed. "It's ok, I was just thinking."

"I'm not sure if you heard, but Laquó and Luther were discussing our route for tomorrow. Laquó wants to skip the Charno Territory and Luther thinks we should stick to the original schedule."

"Tomorrow is a new day. Maybe Laquó will change his mind with the new dawn."

"Maybe. I think Shine is about to hand out some Lojo Dolls, and rumour has it, that Serenity has a stash of wheat whiskey. Will you stay with us a little longer around the campfire tonight? That's two very good reasons to steal your company."

"I already have six good reasons." said Tremendous.

"And you make the seventh." said Carmen, taking Tremendos' hand. Tremendos was flooded with an overwhelming feeling of love. Her eyes fill with tears.

"Are you ok, Tremendos?" asked Carmen, worriedly. "I'm so sorry, I should have asked if it was ok to touch your hand."

"Don't apologise," said Tremendos, "I've never felt better."

The sensation was so strong that Tremendos was secretly pleased that Carmen removed her hand from hers. Tremendos' mind was filled with a million images. The images were powerful, euphoric and engulfing, but also so overwhelming that it made her feel faint. "Let's get that wheat whiskey flowing." Carmen nodded, then smiled and ran back to Shine to help distribute the Lojo Dolls.

CHAPTER ELEVEN
JUDGE 1: Tomms Day of Fraz County

The group had packed everything up just before dawn. They started walking as the suruplight rose. By lunchtime, they were only twenty miles away from Charno Territory. They stopped in the woods for a picnic lunch. They would have to restock their supplies in Charno tonight.

Colonius made his way up a large tree with massive extending branches. Laquó, who normally liked to sit alone for meals, decided to join him. Tremendos sat on the picnic blanket with Carmen, Luther and Shine. Serenity had found a pond and was skimming stones. She had found a quite brilliant skimming stone on the walk this morning. She was eager to try it out. After using up all her smaller ones, which skimmed alright, she pulled out the larger, flatter stone. She took a deep breath and applied lots of thrust behind her skimming wrist-flick. The stone went so far that it hit a tree on the other side of the pond. It made a loud knocking sound that ricocheted through the forest. A moment passed. She heard the sound again, and then again. The noise had now caught the attention of the whole group.

"Can you tell where it's coming from?" Luther shouted up to Colonius and Laquó in the tree.

"Yes," replied Laquó, "there's a man further down. He's working on a totem pole."

On hearing this, Shine stood up, mid-sandwich. She called up to Laquó. "Laquó, can you come with me please? I want to say hello."

There was a ruffle in the group. Had Shine felt something, sensed something? Shamans were taught that their intuition was their best friend. They should always listen to it, but not necessarily always follow it. Laquó climbed down from the tree and made his way towards Shine. The two walked over to the man, whilst the others went back to their lunch and stone-skimming.

The man they saw was Tomms Day. He was a carpenter from Charno Territory. He saw the two Shamans approaching and put down his chisel and hammer.

After about thirty minutes, Luther stood up and peered over towards the totem pole. The man had started working on the totem pole again. He could see Laquó and Shine sitting on the ground watching him work.

"It can't be that easy, surely." Luther said to himself.

Overhearing him, Serenity replied. "Hey, if these Judges want to come to us, rather than us go to them - I'm fine with that." Tremendos and Luther laughed. Colonius came down from the tree to join them. "I've just seen Shine remove a copy of the Journals from her satchel. I think he could be our first Judge!"

The rest of The Collective stood up and peered over towards Tomms Days.

"Well, that was fast," said Serenity, "one night in the forest and the Universe delivers."

Tremendos chipped in, "It was meant to be, clearly."

"Are there nine more of you in these woods?" Serenity shouted out to the trees. The Collective laughed.

Later that night, around midlight, The Collective are sat around the campfire discussing the next day's schedule.

"Do we need to head to Charno Territory now?" asked Laquó. Tremendos looked over at him, knowing full well that Laquó didn't want to go there.

"Well, we have to head North anyway, to get to Ozro. Bypassing Charno would save us a good few days. Tremendos, what's your insight on this, should we proceed to Charnos?"

Tremendos took a sip of gingero tea and pulled out her golden book.

"From the moment you found Tomms, I've been having visions of various Ozro landmarks. My instinct says there are no more Judges to be found here in Fraz. It'll take us about six weeks to reach the border anyway if we go via the faster route and bypass Charno. That's plenty of time to keep our eyes open and be vigilant, as we always would be."

"Thanks, Tremendos. Ok, let's vote. Those in favour of by-passing Charno and just heading straight to the Fraz-Ozro border say 'Koli'." Luther received six echoes of 'Koli', it was unanimous.

"Great. It's decided then. Tomorrow we head North-West of Charno and up over the Galatacan Mountains and towards the border."

The Collective said goodnight and headed to their tents. Carmen asked Shine to hold back by the campfire, saying that she wanted to talk to her about something.

"How do you feel, about today I mean?" asked Carmen.

"Good, I feel good. We knew immediately we had our Judge. When Tomms started working, it just confirmed it. Limitless amounts of patience and such a solid virtue about his work. He's been a carpenter for around thirteen years. Prior to the Pilgrimage, I'd been having a re-occurring dream about a wooden totem pole. I could see its key features. When we met Tomms, he was halfway through a feature. I couldn't quite make it out. Watching him work was blissful. So much care, so much attention. When he finished the feature, it was exactly as I'd seen it my dream."

"Predominus. Wow, that's cool."

"Am quite interested in predominus abilities. Have been working closely with Cressida to develop it."

"That's great Shine!" Carmen gave Shine a hug. "Shine, I have to tell you something and I'm just going to come out and say it."

"Yes?"

"I'm in love with you."

Carmen couldn't see it, but Shine's cheeks had started to burn, and it wasn't from the campfire flames.

"Ok, let me see...I wasn't expecting you to say that."

"I don't believe in beating around the bush on these things. I like to be direct. To be honest, I didn't think I'd have the courage to tell you, but..."

"Wait, was that you who sent me the stone message?" Carmen nodded. "And was it you who sent me those Gojine plants seeds?" Carmen nodded.

"Shine, I've been in love with you from the first moment I saw you. I value our friendship more than anything in the world, but I had to tell you. You're my best friend and it feels strange keeping secrets from you."

"I understand. Carmen…," Shine looked Carmen in the eye. Carmen's eyes had filled up with tears.

"Carmen, I am so sorry, but I don't know what to make of this. I love you, as a friend, but to be in love? Well, we have so much to do on this Pilgrimage…I'm not sure we have the time to explore this…I…"

"It's ok, Shine. I can see this has come as quite a shock. I thought you may have already known it, but obviously not. Look, please don't feel any pressure to feel one way or another. Just take this information and let it settle. I'm in love with you. I don't think that will ever change. However, if you don't feel the same way, well…then the onus is on me to find a way to keep our beautiful friendship going. I hope you feel that's possible. I cherish it and honour it. If you reject me, I will find a way to move on. It'll be hard, but I'll have to find a place to shelf my romantic feelings towards you."

"Thank you, Carmen. Your honesty and friendship are what I value most in this world, always know that. I think I need to go to bed and sleep. Goodnight, Carmen."

Shine gave Carmen a hug and walked off to her tent.

Carmen watched her go. She kicked some wood near the fire. *I really hope I've not blown our friendship.*

In her tent that night, Shine couldn't sleep. She tossed and turned and then, eventually, she started to cry. She cried and cried. It was uncontrollable. She thought her eyelids might dry up completely. *What is wrong with me? Why am I breaking my heart right now?* Shine didn't know it yet, but the reason she was crying so much was because she couldn't believe that she was worthy of someone's love. Shine did have feelings for Carmen but accepting Carmen's love would mean accepting that she was worthy of it, and that wasn't something that she couldn't quite get her head around just yet.

CHAPTER TWELVE
JUDGE 2: Ignacius Prime of Ozro

The Collective stuck to the plan. They spent six weeks heading North-West towards the Ozro border. There were no clues, no hints, and no signs of another potential Judge in Fraz County. Tremendos had been right. In fact, Tremendos had found it quite humorous that the Universe should gift them with their first Judge on the second day of the Pilgrimage. That Judge had been delivered to them, but of course, they would spend the next month and a half finding nothing at all. Searching for Judges was just like searching for gold nuggets. Lots of patience and perseverance was required.

The Collective had been in Ozro for a week. They had decided to head straight to Ipa first, in the Northern Territory. After that, they planned to work their way around the suburbs and coastline. The journey to Ipa had taken most of the full week. It was their first official day in the capital. The Collective were in a market bazaar in the Grassmarket trading post. They were playing a game of Zoto with some locals. The Grassmarket was a distinctly pleasant market compared to others in Ozro or other countries. It was always busy, and locals took diligent care of the streets and stalls. As he waited his turn at the Zoto table, Luther's attention fell upon a vegetable stall across from them. It wasn't the stall that had caught his focus, it was the monkey-moom sitting in a cage far too small for a monkey-moom. Luther was unsettled by this.

Zoto is a four-player game. Two teams of two play against each other. Massive orange die determine the game, along with strategy and card tactics. Shine had never understood the game all that well. She was paired up with Serenity. Serenity loved Zoto and was quite skilled at it. As the two discussed tactics against a cattle-selling father and son duo, Carmen watched Shine, and the game, with anticipation. Shine had seemed quite distant in recent weeks. It was to be expected, thought Carmen. For now, Carmen was stepping back. She hoped, dearly, that Shine would accept her love. If she couldn't, then she hoped that, at the very least, they go back to something resembling their normal friendship.

Colonius and Laquó were discussing Zoto tactics and what they might do when it came to their turn. They would play whoever won the game between the cattle sellers and the Shamans. Luther was still transfixed on the monkey-moom. He approached Tremendos. "Can you help me with something?"

Tremendos looked up from her golden book. "Yes, of course."

"Do you see that monkey-moom over there? The one in the tiny cage?"

"Yes, I see him."

"Could you tell me a little bit about how he got there?" Tremendos nodded and stood up. She wandered nonchalantly to the vegetable stall, pretending to look at the selection on display. She touched the cage and concentrated. She got an instant flashback. The monkey-moom had been at the stall, trying to steal some vegetables to eat. The stall owner had tried to catch him on a few occasions - one day he did.

He'd kept him in the cage ever since. The veg owner had a stern face and big black eyebrows that sat on his brow like two menacing furrypillars. Tremendos headed back to Luther. By this point, Colonius had taken an interest in what was happening across the road too. He left Laquó to watch the table. Tremendos told Luther and Colonius what she saw. Just then, a tall man with a head full of black raven hair and a cream suit walked over to the veg stall. He had a canary-yellow bow tie and deep brown eyes. He pushed his small round black glasses back on his face and looked around. He asked the stall owner for something. The stall owner walked to the other side of the stall to retrieve the man's request. Certain the owner was now distracted, the tall man tried to discretely open the cage. The monkey- moom was scared. He refused to come out of the cage and started to make some screeching noises. The veg owner heard this and ran over to the tall man. He started shouting at him and threw a pack of vegetables at him. Without even thinking on it, Colonius ran across the busy market street to intervene. He told the veg stall owner how he'd witnessed a young boy open the cage and that the tall man was just trying to close it over. Colonius produced a piece of paper from his breast pocket. He quickly flashed it in front of the veg owner. He told him that he was from animal control and that he needs to see the permit for the monkey-moom. The veg owner grew increasingly angry and started shouting and making a scene.

The group had, by now, stopped playing, and were watching the scenario unfold across the road.

Luther and Carmen ran across to assist. The veg owner had a ripe tomaten aimed at the tall man's head and was shouting obscenities at Colonius. Luther stepped in and tries to talk to the veg owner. Carmen took the tall man's arm and walked him back across the road, out of harm's way. Colonius took a step back. He watched as Luther handed the veg owner some money. The veg owner quietens down and motions for them to get away from his veg stall. Colonius stepped back in, lifted the cage, closed the door over and said,

"We're taking this."

The veg owner glared at Colonius, who just glared back at him. Colonius, Luther and the monkey-moom headed back to the group. Carmen had got the tall man a drink. She took a seat next to him. Colonius sat at the other side of him.

"Are you alright?" asked Colonius.

The man was a little shaken. He took a sip of his drink.

"I'm fine, thank you, thank you."

"Do you know this monkey-moom?" asked Carmen. "No, not at all. I just know that the cage is too small. That man is mean. I have to walk past his stall every day. The injustice of it was killing me. I couldn't just let it happen."

Colonius pointed to Luther. "It was my friend over there that first spotted the same." Luther waved from the other side of the table. He had taken Colonius' place at the Zoto table and was now playing alongside Laquó against the cattle–sellers.

Tremendos walked over to Carmen, Colonius and the tall man. "Would you mind if I took the monkey-moom? I have a friend near here who will be able to find it a loving home."

"Please, yes, of course, that sounds great." said the tall man.

"I'm Carmen," Carmen extended her hand for a high three.

"Ignatius." replied the tall man, giving her, Colonius and Tremendos a high three.

Tremendos took the monkey-moom and started to walk away. Colonius could hear her talking to it. The tall man took a breath and sifted his large hands through his jet-black hair.

"I still feel a bit shaky somehow, not sure why."

Carmen and Colonius looked at each other and smiled.

"There's a booth over there, at the back of this market. Can we buy you some food?"

"Maybe something to eat would be good, but please, let me buy us something - my way of saying thank you for saving me from a tomaten pelting!"

Carmen and Colonius laughed and nodded. The three of them headed over to the booth.

After placing their order with the market waiter, their cold and minty Dilli drinks arrived first. Dilli drinks were a popular tonic drink made from Gojine berries, apfel water and mint. It was a refreshing drink, and very good for the calming of nerves.

"Happy Travelling!" said Carmen.

"Happy Travelling!" replied Colonius and Ignacius.

"I'm going to get to the point, Ignacuis. Colonius and I, and our friends over there, are Shamans. Tremendos, that lady in the grey gown, she's a Visionary."

Ignacuis moved his thick, black-rimmed glasses back onto his face. He took a sip of Dilli, his eyes absolutely focused on Carmen's every word.

"We're on a Pilgrimage, you may have heard of it?"

"Yes, yes, I have."

"And you know who we are looking for?"

"The founding Supreme Judges for Venezeli."

"That's right." said Colonius. "What do you do for a living?"

"I'm a Professor at M.U.C."

"We're going to level with you Ignacius," said Carmen, "you have heart, a lot of heart."

"We've known you less than an hour - I can already tell that you have a wise and measured head on your shoulders too. You have perspective."

"Well that's very kind of you, but if I had good perspective, I would have had a better rescue plan for that monkey-moon!" Ignacius joked, "And I didn't foresee that veg seller's reaction." Ignacius took another sip of minty Dilli drink. Hints of lavender came through. He could feel the tonic calm him down.

"That's where your heart came in," said Carmen, "and Colonius is right, you have a decent quality about you - a desire for the greater good of others, even monkey-mooms."

"You're asking me to be a Judge?"

Colonius nodded and Carmen smiled. "As you know," said Colonius, "those chosen need to have a strong reason to decline the offer."

"I'm aware of that."

"How do you feel about it?"

"Am not sure. I mean it's an absolute honour, but what if I can't perform?"

"Everyone we choose will think that. Anyone who doesn't have any fear, trepidation or doubts isn't right for the job anyway."

Colonius took something out of his bag. "There are many people and resources at your disposal." he re-assured, "Today, here and now, we are going to entrust you with your own abridged copy of the legislative directives from the Prophetic Journals," Ignacius almost spat out his Dilli drink.

"You will receive monthly updates directly from the administrative team in Ipa, as well as monthly calls from our contacts in Ipa and Fraz County. The Koli Ceremony will take place around two weeks after we find the last Judge on planet Jenar. You and the Judges will have a further twelve months from that point to learn and develop in your roles."

A tear came to Ignatius' eye. It started to sink in.
"Do you have family, here in Ipa?" asked Carmen.
"Yes, yes, I do."
"Well, you're one of the lucky ones then. You will be given a large residence for you and your family in Ipa, in the Judges' quarters. You don't have to move countries. Most of the other Judges will have to."

"Thank you." said Ignacuis. "I became a Professor to help others, to do good. This is an opportunity to continue that path. I accept, I accept."

"Fantastic!" exclaimed Carmen. The waiter returned with their food and the trio spend the rest of the afternoon talking and answering Ignacius' questions.

"Before we go," said Carmen, "this is a gift, from our coven leader." Carmen pulled out the circular fern-shaped amulet and handed it to Ignacius.

Ignacius took it off her, kissed it, and placed it in his pocket.

"Thank you."

"It's for good luck on your journey." said Carmen.

"Read the journals," advised Colonius, "be available for the updates and we will see you in around a year's time, maybe sooner." The Shamans said their goodbyes and headed back to their Inn lodgings in Ipa's bustling marketplace.

CHAPTER THIRTEEN
JUDGE 3: Lara Trinkett of Ozro

"This is a Pilgrimage, Serenity, not a bus holiday!" Laquó stormed out of the main food tent and headed straight towards his tent.

"Wait! Laquó, hear me out!" said Serenity as she ran out after him. "We've been on foot for around what, ten weeks now? My calves are on fire! Am fairly sure there's nothing in the Prophetic Journals that says we can't have a van."

Serenity followed Laquó into his tent.

"That may be so," said Laquó as he busily folded and re-folded his clothes, "however it's not the way."

"Laquó, our main objective remains the same. We can still observe in the more populated areas. The van is merely for those stretches we know have nothing but rocks, hills, trees, coastline and mountains."

"We'll put it to a vote."

Later that night, by their campfire, the vote resulted in three for and three against. Those for the van were Serenity, Colonius and Carmen. Those against were Laquó, Luther and Shine.

"Really Shine?" asked Serenity. Carmen jumped in to defend her.

"She's traditionally minded when it comes to things like this. Don't be hard on her, Serenity, she's entitled to her opinion."

"Where's Tremendos?" asked Serenity, "She has the deciding vote."

Tremendos walked up to the van and inspected it. She touched the bonnet.

"We keep the van." Tremendos took a seat by the campfire.

Colonius stood up, "We should have just asked Tremendos in the first place."

"My visions aren't always right, but my instinct says we keep the van."

The Collective were currently at a lakeside base, a perfect spot for checking out the suburbs of Ipa. They had left Ipa the day after finding Ignacius and decided to head North-East. The base was at Cardinal Lake, which fed into the North Eastern shoreline of Ozro. Serenity had bought the van from a travelling painter she met in the nearby woods. The artist needed the money to move to Ipa. He told Serenity that he planned to sell his work there.

Serenity felt she was doing a good deed for the artist and saving The Collective some time and lactic acid from all their walking. With the van, they could do the perimeter of the shoreline in less than half the time and move on to Zaatta much earlier than anticipated.

After the vote, Carmen and Luther decided to play cards by the campfire. Shine was reading her book. Every now and then, she would secretly look up over the book's edge at Carmen. She loved the way Carmen smiled and laughed. She loved the way her auburn hair curled around her face, and how her fern-green eyes always had a twinkle in them. Her eyes looked like all they could see was love and beauty. Shine hadn't been able to stop thinking about Carmen's proposition. She had tried to focus on her Journals and manuscripts. She spent a lot of time learning about Jimus Krakovia's vision of the prophecy. She practiced her predominus techniques daily and tried to make a few Lojo Dolls every night. No matter how busy she kept, she couldn't avoid the essential question Carmen had put to her. Did she love her? Yes. The answer was yes. Shine did love Carmen, with all her heart. She could think of no one else on the planet she'd rather spend her life with. Was she ready? Did she have what it would take to give that love back in abundance? A few weeks ago, Shine would have said no. Tonight, she felt empowered. She wasn't sure what had changed. Was it a newfound confidence after discovering Tomms in the woods all those weeks ago? Did that event reaffirm something she had been doubting about herself? Why was she so good at spotting things in others, but not in herself? Carmen had kept her promise. She kept her distance since opening her heart to Shine. Shine had appreciated that. The journey itself had given her lots of time to grapple with inner daemons. Shine felt like she had addressed a lot of internal questions. She was still scared as hell but was sure this was normal. Here they were, asking complete strangers to make a complete life change for a greater cause. And here she was, lucky enough to have a brilliant and loving person declaring her love to her forevermore. This was no time for fear. Shine believed she could make Carmen happy, and if she struggled, she would use every day of her life trying her best.

Tremendos and Laquó were collecting driftwood by the lakeside for firewood.

"We're probably going to be here a few days," said Laquó, "we'll have time to dry these out."

Laquó and Tremendos both went, unknowingly, for the same log. Tremendos accidentally brushed her hand across his.

"I'm sorry…" said Tremendos, stepping back quite quickly.

"It's ok," said Laquó, "you can have that log." He smiled at Tremendos, intrigued by her quiet character and calm nature. Tremendos seemed lost, she seemed distant.

"Are you ok?" asked Laquó.

"Yes, yes, am fine thank you." she replied. "This wood will come in handy. There's some bad weather coming soon."

"Oh right," said Laquó with a jokey tone to his voice.

"I'm weatherproofing my tent this evening. I trust you far more than I trust those meteorologists." Laquó laughed. Tremendos still looked shaken. Laquó knew - she saw something when she touched his hand. She must have.

Carmen noticed Shine looking at her from behind her book. She excused herself from her card game with Luther. Shine delved her nose back into her book.

"Shine, would you like to go for a walk?"

Shine nodded and stood up. "Yes."

The woods nearby were well lit from a low, peach-coloured light. It filled the sky with a warm haze this evening. There was a slight chill in the air.

"Here," said Carmen, "take my coat."

"Thank you," replied Shine. "In fact, I want to thank you for a lot of things."

"What for?" asked Carmen.

"Your patience has been great and…well…"

Shine lunged forward and kissed Carmen. Carmen was stunned at first, then relaxed. She brought Shine into her arms. Shine was nervous as hell. She didn't know what compelled her to kiss Carmen, but it felt like the right thing to do. Shine melted into Carmen's arms. She felt relaxed now, but her heart felt like it was beating at a thousand beats a minute.

"I love you, Carmen. I just wasn't sure I deserved your love - but I think I do."

"Yes, you do. I am blessed to have yours." Carmen and Shine took each other's hands. The tree canopy above them looked like it might envelop them both with a branchy hug full of joy. The suruplight was quickly fading and midlight was on its way out.

"Shall we tell the others?" asked Carmen.

"Absolutely." replied Shine.

Shine and Carmen met The Collective around the campfire later that night for supper. The group were laughing, Serenity was telling some jokes and the gingero tea was flowing.

"Guys, we have some news for you." said Shine, standing up.

On hearing the news, The Collective stood and cheered.

They passed out hugs to both Shamans.

"This is a great day!" said Luther. Tremendos hugged Laquó, the first outward act of emotion anyone in the group had witnessed. Tremendos leaned in closer to Laquó. She whispered into his ear.

"You are a man of great integrity. You have a big heart. You are on the right path."

Laquó nodded and smiled. He took Tremendos' hands and gave them a gentle kiss. He took his leave from the group and headed to his tent.

"Is Laquó alright?" asked Carmen.

"He's going to be fine." replied Tremendos. "Just fine."

***

The Collective rose early the following day to do some group meditation. They sat in a circle, around the campfire spot, and held hands whilst Luther led the meditation. The focus of the session was renewed energy. The group anticipated they were about a fifth of the way through their journey. They still had nine Judges to find. They called upon the power of the surup, the lunar and the whole Universe that morning. Luther finished the session off with a congratulatory message for Carmen and Shine. The women were happier than ever. Both felt renewed in their work and their personal lives.

The Collective had breakfast then started to tidy up around their camp. Serenity went to start the van. Her plan was to give it a run around the clearing and warm the engine before it made its way along the coastline. Her plan didn't work. The van absolutely, positively would not start. Serenity made her way back to the group. "We have a problem." she said, sheepishly.

The group quickly understood the situation. Colonius looked under the bonnet. "All of the best mechanics are back in Ipa."

Serenity put on her top robe. "It's a beautiful, surupy day. Anyone fancy a walk back into Ipa?"

Laquó rolled his eyes. Tremendos went over to the van and inspected it. "We'll all go." she said. Her tone wasn't bossy. It was never bossy. It was just knowing. No one even disputed it. The Collective got ready to return to the Metropolis for a mechanic.

As the group made their way back towards Ipa, Shine took Carmen's hand.

"I'll miss our long walks." she said.

"There are still plenty more walks to have." replied Carmen.

***

The market was bustling as The Collective made their way into the busy streets.

"There's one!" shouted Colonius, spotting a garage sandwiched between a florist and a q-nuts vendor. The sign read 'Lara's Garage.' The Collective headed inside. Tremendos stopped dead in her tracks. She was hit by a bright and pressing flashback, a metallic sound screeched in her ears, it almost made her stumble. She paused, then carried on inside.

The garage looked empty. There were plenty of carriages, vehicles and bikes around, but no Lara. The Collective suddenly heard wheels slide out from underneath a car in front of them. It was Lara Trinkett. The six Shamans and Visionary looked down at her. Lara was covered in motor oil. She wiped her brow and Tremendos noticed the large hunket-clench in Lara's hand. Tremendos smiled. Lara stared back up at them.

"Let's see. Seven folk in robes and no vehicle. Am I in some kind of trouble?"

***

Lara had three spare places in her truck. The Collective drew straws. Luther, Serenity and Tremendos won the ride back. Colonius, Laquó, Carmen and Shine were in for another long trek.

"So, you're on a Pilgrimage?" asked Lara.

Tremendos and Serenity were in the back seat. Tremendos had a curious fascination with Lara that she couldn't put her finger on.

"Yes, that's right."

Luther was in the front seat. "So, are you a full-time mechanic?" he asked.

"I have my own garage, but I also like inventing things. Not to brag, but I've been headhunted to help on the MEW5 taskforce. They want me to engineer some of the technologies we might be using. Personally, it's a great honour to help the cause."

Tremendos smiled and jotted something down in her golden book. Serenity was impressed with Lara's story.

"That's so cool!" she said, patting Lara on the back. Lara blushed.

"Well, you know, I just want to do my bit."

***

Colonius and Laquó were walking a little bit ahead of Carmen and Shine. The Shamans had held back so that they could talk privately. Shine went into her pocket. "I bought you something, at the market." She handed Carmen a small item wrapped in crepe paper.

"I wanted to get this for you the first time we were in Ipa but didn't. Given that we were given a second opportunity to go there, I took it this time."

Carmen smiled and accepted the gift.

"Thank you Shine. This is wonderful." She unraveled the paper layers. It was a bronze necklace chain with a small bronze pocket watch on the end.

"Time is eternal, and so is love. It's us who are transient. This is why we always strive to make the most of both."

"I love it Shine! Thank you so much!" Carmen gave Shine a kiss and a hug.

"You know, I still have that note you sent me, the night before we left."

"You do?" asked Carmen.

"I don't know why, but I folded it up and kept it here, in my locket, so that I could keep it close to me. I didn't even know who it was from back then. Isn't that silly?"

"It's not silly at all. I think it's lovely, just like you."

Carmen took Shine's hand, and they carried on walking through the forest.

***

Midlight had fallen when the rest of the group got back to camp. Luther had started cooking for the group. Lara had started work on the van. Lara was assisted by her new apprentice, Serenity, who was handing her tools and helping. Tremendos was sitting on a nearby rock, looking pensive. She watched as Lara worked away. Lara was meticulous and careful. Tremendous could see that she was also quite brilliant at thinking on her feet. It was as if Lara was already ten steps ahead of the next problem waiting to show itself. The van started to purr. Tremendos saw Lara and Serenity have a celebratory high three.

***

The group were eagerly and appreciatively enjoying Luther's home-cooked meal. Tremendos walked over to Lara and sat beside her. "May I speak with you?"

"Yes, of course." replied Lara. She put down her finished plate on the log seat and grabbed a bottle of beer. Lara stood up. The two of them headed away from the campfire for a walk.

"I think you'd be very helpful at MEW5." said Tremendos. The pair were walking along the lakeside. There was a chill in the air. Tremendos put her hands inside her robe pouch. This made her look even more pensive and Zen-like.

"Thank you." replied Lara.

"Have you considered that there might be an even higher calling for you?"

"What do you mean?"

"You know we're looking for ten Judges from Venezeli?"

"Yes." Lara took a sip of her beer.

"I think you are one of them," Lara spat her beer out in surprise.

"I'm so sorry about that. Did you just say...me?"

"Yes, Lara. You have a grounded foresight. You don't jump to conclusions. You analyse, you inspect, you assess – all this helps you see clearly. You solve problems. That's what the best Judges do – they solve problems. They use a just hand and a measured mind to find resolutions."

"But I'm just a mechanic."

"No Lara. You're just a Judge with extra skills. Do you have a sound reason not to accept?"

"Not really, no."

Tremendos pulled a book out of her pouch. "Then here, read this. Make it your day and night.

Make plans for your garage, a successor. You have been chosen Lara. You're lucky, you will have more time than the others to brush up on all of this. More time to get your affairs in order. We will send you funds and information on exactly what to do and when."

"What about my family?"

"There will be new lodgings for you and your family in the Judges' quarter of Ipa, rent free. And trust me, it will be better than any of those run-down shacks that thief Thackery rented out over the years."

"You know Thackery?"

"No, but I know you bought your truck from him. That truck is still filled with memories of his misdeeds and bad deals. It was quite unpleasant."

"I should exorcise my truck of bad Koli." laughed Lara.

"A good cleansing wouldn't be a bad idea. If only you knew a Shaman who could help you out…" winked Tremendos. Lara laughed. The pair had almost done a full circuit one of the smaller lakes near the base.

"You can ask us any questions you like tonight, specific details, whatever you want to know. The rest will come to you over the coming months."

"Thank you, Tremendos."

"You're going to be a terrific Judge – so, thank you, in advance."

CHAPTER FOURTEEN
JUDGE 4: Bird Night of Zaatta

Tremendos was sure The Collective had found all the Judges they were going to find in Ozro. She advised they move on. The others agreed. Zaatta was calling next, and that's where they would head to tomorrow. The Collective said goodbye to Lara in the morning. They were now heading South, in their newly repaired and fully functioning minivan. The group found the van to be wonderfully comfortable for a van of its age. There was plenty of room for luggage - luggage they had been carrying on their backs for weeks. The boot door transformed into a mini-kitchen counter, which pleased Luther no end.

Zaatta was the only country in Venezeli that shared a border with all the other countries. It was right in the centre of the planet's only continent. This meant that it was surrounded by other four countries and had no coastline or sea. Zattaa took its border control very seriously.

The Collective had made its way through border police swiftly. They came in from the North and spent two weeks around Toffenpost. There were lots of schools and orphanages in the village of Toffenpost. The Collective visited them all. It wasn't just adults who could be Judges. Children with particular insight were also eligible. Toffenpost was famous for its goldmines. Gold mining was a dangerous field of work on Venezeli. The cave walls were fragile and over-mining made them even more so. Unfortunately, there had been many accidents in the Northern Territory mines over the last hundred years. This left a lot of orphaned children.

The Collective didn't get much of a feeling for Toffenpost, so they headed South, towards Stoffenlaggen. The plan was to do an overnight stay in a diner-motel stop-off, then carry on inland towards the Andanuan forest.

The diner-motel was pleasant enough. The Collective had dropped off their luggage in their motel rooms and were in the diner for something to eat. It was quiet season, so The Collective managed to get their own rooms. Carmen and Shine decided to share, nonetheless.

They had ordered seven large dough-breads with some crispy pot-pots to share on the side.

"Well, that's one find each for Laquó, Shine, Colonius, Tremendos and Carmen." Serenity lifted the peffer pot and put it to her mouth like a microphone, "Will any of them make it to two finds this month?" She moved the peffer pot over to Colonius, waiting for an answer. He shoved it away and laughed.

"And will me and Luther ever leave the starting line?"

"It's not a competition, Serenity. You do know that?" said Shine with a smile.

"But it is!" said Serenity, "I have a barrel of firecracker wheat whiskey riding on my win! Place your bets now." The group laughed and tucked into their delicious hot meal.

The food went down a treat. Serenity needed to make a restroom stop. "Someone check out what strudels they have please!" she said as she stood to find the restroom. The Collective were sitting in a separate backroom of the diner, the front booths and diner bar were filled with locals this evening. As Serenity walked into the front of the diner, she spotted a waitress talking to, what looked like, a truck driver.

"Come on Jerry," the waitress pleaded, "you know we reserve this booth for Chuck every Montag evening. This is his booth. Him and Mary used to sit here all the time."

"Well, Mary isn't here anymore. But I am, and I want my Koli-damned Kaffee!" The trucker man banged his fist down on the table.

Serenity saw the waitress put her pad and pen away in her apron and take a deep breath.

"Jerry, I'm not asking you. I'm telling you. You cannot sit here. And talking to me in that tone of voice is certainly not going to get you your Kaffee any quicker, is it now?"

Her tone was delicate, but firm. Serenity liked this woman. She asserted authority, firmness, but with lashings of charm and fairness. A bar stool became available. Serenity, intrigued to see what would happened next, took a seat. The restroom could wait a couple of minutes more, she was sure of that.

The trucker man didn't move. He glared at the waitress. The waitress stood her ground. "Jerry, this is the last time I'll ask nicely. Now, you're lucky I'm not a vindictive person, because if I was, I could make sure to put some real nasty things in your Kaffee every day from here on in. But I wouldn't do that, would I?"

The trucker man huffed and stood up. It was clear he had been drinking.

"Now you come and sit over here, right in this booth here," said the waitress, guiding the man to his new seat.

"Thank you, Jerry."

Jerry huffed again, then lay his head down on the table. He must have thought his head was as light as a feather, but it wasn't. It landed on the table with a thud.

"I'll be right there with your Kaffee!" said the waitress as she glided back towards the bar counter. Serenity saw this as her cue to quickly go to the restroom. Upon returning, she took a seat at the bar counter again, eagerly awaiting the arrival of Chuck.

The waitress had put two place settings on the empty booth by the window. She'd put a candle in the centre and some flowers by the condiments.

Chuck, an older and happy looking fellow, came through the door in a knitted vest and a brown shirt. He had big blue eyes and a wide caring smile.

"Bird!" he called out to the waitress. "How nice to see

you!"

"Chuck!," replied the waitress, her grin spread from ear to ear. "I'll be right with you Chuck, please, take a seat."

The waitress returned and handed Chuck a menu. "I'll give you a few moments Chuck. Usual drink though?" Chuck nodded in delight. Bird, the waitress, knew that Chuck would order the exact same thing that he'd been ordering since the diner first opened twenty-five years ago. He and his wife, Mary, used to frequent the diner every Montag evening. They had a table by the window, every time, at the same time. They ordered the same meal and the same drinks every week, but they always like to look at the menu, just in case something from the specials caught their eye. It never did. It had been two years since Mary died, but Chuck still came to the diner, every Montag evening, every week. Bird set a place for her, always. She would use her tips to buy fresh flowers for Chuck's table, every Montag.

Serenity spent a long time looking at Bird. She had a kind smile and a caring nature. Shine appears next to Serenity and tapped her on the shoulder. "Hey there, we thought you'd got lost in the restrooms."

"Look at this lady, Shine. What do you think?"
"The waitress?" enquired Shine.

"Yes." said Serenity

Shine studied her for a minute. "Well, I think she probably has the patience of a saint."

"That's exactly what I was thinking." said Serenity. "Come with me, would you Shine?" Serenity stood up and went over to Bird.

"Excuse me, miss?"

"Yes?" Bird's smile melted both Serenity and Shine's Shamanic hearts. This was a person who could see good and do good and be perfectly measured alongside it. Someone who fought for justice whilst keeping their calm, Someone who couldn't be bought or manipulated.

"Is your boss around?" asked Serenity, "We may need a

minute of your time."

***

The Collective looked on from inside the diner as Shine and Serenity talked to Bird outside. The Shamans were sitting on a bench whilst Bird perched on an old fruit cart.

"Just two weeks in Zaatta and we have our fourth Judge already. Not bad." said Carmen.

"I have a feeling there's at least one more in Zaatta," said Tremendos, "but don't ask me where or when."

"Would it be ok if we pay a visit to the Zaattan monks?" asked Colonius. "It's been a long time since I've visited - I think we could all do with a bit of personal care and self-reflection time. Re-charge our batteries. The monks are amazing hosts. We could do some voluntary work for them in return if you don't mind?"

"Well, that also wasn't on the original schedule," said Laquó, sounding irritated, "but I guess we can put it to a vote." He smiled. Laquó had grown fond of Colonius, who had managed to mellow his temper.

It was decided. The group would make their way through the Andanuan forest for some well-needed self-care at the Monastery. After that, The Collective would head to the small village towns in and around the greater Andanuan area. Zaattan's medical district wasn't far from there. The medical district had some of Venezeli's best medical students and staff. The Andanuan forest was rich in minerals and complex biological organisms. This made Zaatta the perfect research base for anyone in the medical profession.

The night that Serenity and Shine found Bird, The Collective had a full night of celebration. They danced with Stoffenlaggen locals in the diner until the early hours. They eat and drank and laughed and had a very deep sleep the following morning. Upon waking, The Collective got re-hydrated, went for a short walk around the motel, read, slept some more and eat hearty food. The following day, they would be leaving the van on the outskirts of the forest and venturing deep into the Andanuan plane.

There were two main threats in the Andanuan forest: Crosantian snakes and Zaattan bears. Neither were friendly or sociable. In fact, the former was deadly, and the latter was so big it would scare you to death first. The Shamans were prepared. They had anti-venom for the worst-case scenario with the snakes and they would just have to take their chances with the Zaattan bears.

Crosantian snakes were yellow and black. Their skin colours mixed together like a marbled pebble. They were long, extraordinarily long. Nobody knew just how long they were. No-one had ever kept a Crosantian snake in captivity, but someone had managed to collect some venom for scientists to make anti-venom. Other than that, the snakes were left alone to go about their business. They had a ferocious bite that could kill in less than a minute. They smelled of burnt orange skin - this was the first sign they were near.

Zaattan bears could fly. They had to take a good run first to sum up the momentum for lift off - but fly they could. They are around two metres wide and five and a half metres tall. They are fiercely protective of their young cubs. When they think their cubs are in danger, they won't think twice about attacking. They don't have the best temperaments at the best of times – they're a very angry bear species. They are black in colour with multi-coloured strands on their coats. They smell of lavender. They have small faces and large sharp teeth and claws.

The Collective were deep in the Andanuan forest now. They started at the edge and were working their way through. It was a long way to the

Monastery, but this was the only way to get there. The monks lived at the foot of the Zaattan Mounties. It was frightening making your way through this forest. The trees seemed over a mile tall. It was dark for most of the journey. The sound of forest animals was petrifying.

In the future, Venezelians would be able to fly, but these were the years before the invention of gravitational flight chips. Gravitational flight chips revolutionised the way in which Venezelian's travelled. Before this discovery, they could not fly. Clever technology involving gravitational magnetism and brain hardwiring meant that a chip in the ankle and the wrist could change all that. But that was still years away. The Collective would have to walk their way through the Andanuan forest, they didn't have the luxury of flying over it.

Carmen thought the forest was beautiful. She marveled at the glowing metallic colours that washed over rocks and gleamed in the water. It tinted everything it touched. The forest grew darker the further they ventured into it. If they attuned their eyes around torchlight, there was so much colour, life and beauty to see. The thing that Carmen loved most was the colour of the trees. Each strand on each branch looked like fibre optic coloured pine needle. Carmen stopped walking. "Guys, I smell burnt orange."

"Everyone stay very still." said Colonius. He walked towards Carmen. "Carmen, very slowly, without turning around, please walk backwards for me, one step at a time – get behind me." Carmen did as instructed.

"Ok everyone. I see the snake, he's about two metres away. He's at two o'clock, right in front of me. On three, I want everyone to point their torches at him. These snakes are sensitive to light. It won't be able to attack. He should turn away."

The Collective got their torches ready.

"One…two…three!"

It worked. The snake jumped back as if shot, then turned and slithered away.

"Well done Colonius!" said Serenity. "That was great."

"Only twenty-five more miles of forest to go." joked Colonius. "Trust me though, it's going to be worth it."

It was dark when The Collective arrived at the foothills of the Monastery. The group had been travelling in darkness for most of the day. To emerge to suruplight would have damaged their eyes.

They saw five little huts ahead of them, and one larger one in the distance. Gas lamps lit all the porches aglow.

"We're here." said Colonius, smiling from ear to ear. The Collective's stay with the monks was every bit as rewarding as Colonius had promised. The monk's leader was Master Monk Kalista. Kalista was a young girl from one of the nearby villages. One day, she had an accident in a waterfall at the edge of her village. She had dived from the waterfall to save a young boy from drowning. In doing so, she almost drowned herself. Kalista survived, however when she came to, the old Kalista was gone. In her place was an old and ancient spirit. The spirit still recognised everyone that Kalista knew. The spirit had merged with Kalista's soul and personality; however, this was a re-born Kalista. She had wisdom beyond her years, knowledge that someone of her age could not possibly possess. The fourteen-year-old made her way to the Monastery. At that time, it was led by Master Monk Bahara. Bahara took Kalista in. He taught her the ways of the Monastery. When Bahara died, at his request, Kalista was to take his place.

Kalista had not aged a day since the accident. That was one hundred and three years ago. The monks were not sure if Kalista could ever die or be killed. She wasn't sure of it either, but if she ever did, she knew it would be her soul to die first, not her young body.

Kalista had gone out of her way to make sure that The Collective were comfortable and had everything they needed. Mornings would start with group meditation in the woods, followed by an afternoon of free time. The monks and The Collective would eat their evening meal together. The monks had started building extensions to the original huts and were planting foundations for a shrine-room, something Kalista was excited about. "I've already seen it," she said, "it will be so beautiful. The monks and I will be able to do all of our finest work there, whilst looking out onto the treetops."

Everyone was incredibly happy to see Colonius again. Colonius was sad to hear that two of the monks he knew had sadly passed away since he left the Monastery. Colonius and Kalista did a special remembrance vigil for them. Days were spent bathing in the monk's home-made pool, rich in Andanuan forest minerals and salts. The Collective would do yoga on the monks' finest Zaattan rugs. They drank the purest and clearest water from the Mountie springs. The visit had been a welcome reparation for The Collective. What wasn't anticipated was how the visit would make Shine feel. Everyone felt re-energised, calm and reconnected with themselves. Shine had felt much more than that. Shine was overwhelmed with gratitude. Something happened to her during her stay with the monks. Something shifted.

She had been bathing in the pool and was looking out over the forest plane. A bird landed by the side of the pool. It looked tiny, fragile and lost. The bird sipped some water, shook its wings and took off. Shine watched as it flew high up over the treetops. She watched on as it soared above the sea of deep forest green. The treetops looked metallic. Thick fern-like leaves swayed gently like a blue-green living thing. Shine knew that further down, the mile-long towering trees became less lush. The darkness made the trees harder and thicker. Down there, the leaves changed from a light ferny green to a dry, pine needle consistency. She concluded it probably had to do with the diminishing suruplight. The bird swooped high. It looked free. It looked brave. Nothing could have prepared Shine for what the bird did next. That tiny bird, so fragile and small, nosedived right into the heart of that forest. And then, just like that, it was gone. Shine didn't realise she was crying. Why did it do that? The dangers, the snakes, the dark. There was a dark sea of unknown in that forest. Who knew what lurked beneath the surface for that little bird? This act of courage struck Shine in the deepest point of her soul. She took a few deep breaths and thought about what she had seen. The bird was living. It lived above and below. If lived fully, without fear. Perhaps it didn't even know how tiny it was. It just lived how it wanted to live. Shine bowed her head and hands towards the forest. She thanked the bird for the lesson it had taught her.

CHAPTER FIFTEEN
JUDGE 5: Zoop Harvey of Zaatta

The Collective spent around two weeks in the small village towns and medical hubs of Zaatta. There were so many selfless individuals at the medical hubs. So many brave, fearless and determined souls, all working to save others. Any number of individuals could have held the qualities for a fine Judge. But the hubs were small. The people near Stoffenlaggen and Toffenpost needed these medics. They admired and gave thanks to the medical staff they encountered. Shine gave out as many Lojo Dolls as she could. There would be no Judges here, their cause was too important. The medics were few and their services were desperately needed in Zattaa.

"I hate to ask, but are your hunches ever wrong, Tremendos?" asked Serenity, "We've spent around eight weeks in Zaatta and no sign of a fifth Judge."

"You're right," replied Tremendos. "Let's head West to Hermos. Am not feeling any further pulls here in Zaatta."

The Collective assembled in their van and started heading West towards the Hermos-Zaattan border. They were on the North end of the border, so that they could head straight to Pinnar City. It was late at night when they approached the border gates. There was no one around the forest clearing or by the gates. Serenity was driving. She decided to pass over the border. As the van's first wheel crossed over into Hermos, a woman's voice belted from a megaphone. "Stop! Stop right there. Don't move any further please. Zaattan border police."

"Oh, great." said Serenity, putting her head into her hands. The Collective looked out the window in confusion. The van was now surrounded by buggy trucks and officers with small pointy hats on.

"Why are we being stopped as we exit Zaatta?" asked Luther. "We had no issues at all coming in."

"Please step out of the van and make an orderly line." A tall woman with a pointy hat was giving the instructions. The combination of the two made her look like a skyscraper in the night sky.

The Collective were escorted to the local Zaattan jailhouse via the multiple buggy trucks.

"What's going on?" asked Serenity.

"All will be discussed at the jailhouse." replied one of the patrol officers.

"Is that really necessary?" asked Colonius.

"We're almost there." replied the officer, re-adjusting his small pointy hat.

The Collective arrived at the jailhouse. Laquó was first to step up to the desk.

"Officer, exactly why are we here?" The tall woman with the megaphone was the Sheriff. She had now removed her pointy hat and was standing on the other side of the desk, inputting some details onto the computer system.

"It's you van, Sir." The Sheriff carried on typing at ferocious speed.

"What about it?" said Serenity, pushing up to the front desk.

"It was reported stolen five week ago."

"I am so sorry, this is my fault." said Serenity, "I bought the van off a guy, around ten weeks ago. He told me he was an artist and that he needed the money to move to Ipa. Said he was going to pursue his career. We needed a van, and he needed the money."

Colonius gave Serenity a hug. "You weren't to know Ser." He addressed the Sheriff.

"If the van was stolen, why did it take so long for anyone to report it? As Serenity mentioned, we've had the van for ten weeks."

"Its owners were on holiday. They only noticed it was gone when they returned home." said the Sheriff. "Could you describe the man who sold you the van?"

"Yes, of course." said Serenity.

"Then come with me." The Sheriff ushered Serenity into a small adjoining room. Before they went in, the Sheriff turned to face The Collective.

"I apologise for any inconvenience. We'll need you to stay here overnight until we can get details of the con artist and get in touch with the van owners. It's not fancy, but you'll be comfortable enough."

The Collective nodded in unison and went back to their open cells and took a seat.

"I'd actually grown quite fond of that van." said Shine, as she wrapped a blanket around herself.

"We can always get another one." said Carmen, as she pulled out a pack of cards. "Anyone for a game?"

"I'm in." said Tremendos without skipping a beat.

"Great!" said Carmen, knowing that weeks ago Tremendos would never have played cards.

"And me." said Colonius.

"I'll play." said Shine.

"Why not." said Laquó, "It's not like there's much else to do. Luther, you playing?"

Luther was watching a young officer on the other side of the jailhouse. The man was handing out meals to some of the other prisoners. "I'm ok, thank you."

"Suit yourself." said Laquó, "What'll it be, Carmen? 'Flying Troops' or 'Jester's Walk' maybe?"

"How about a game of 'Twelve Steps'?"

"Ok! Now we're talking. 'Twelve Steps' it is!" said Laquó.
'Twelve Steps' was a numbers game. It was Laquó's favourite.

Luther continued to watch the young officer as he tended to the prisoners. There was a certain compassion about him. The way he passed out blankets and gave them their food, with care and attention. He had a kind smile.

Carmen was half-way through dealing the deck when the group heard a loud clanging sound coming from one of the cells. It was a drunk man across the jailhouse. He had thrown his plate at the young officer. Just then, Serenity came out of the adjoining room. As she walked past the officer, she stopped to help him pick up the food mess on the floor. Luther stood up and went over to help them.

"Are you alright?" Luther asked the officer. "I saw how hard that plate came flying at you."

The officer laughed. "I'm alright, thank you for asking." He was trying his best to scoop up the tomaten soppen strudel. It was all over him and the floor.

"That's Grito. He's in here most weekends." The officer looked sad, "He doesn't have anyone, so he's always causing chaos around the border. We should really learn to give him solids instead of things like this." Luther and Serenity laughed and continued to help the officer clean up.

"How is your group doing? Is there anything I can do to help you?"

"We're absolutely fine." replied Luther. "Why don't you go freshen up and we'll take care of the rest of this."

"Why thank you, that's very kind of you."

Luther and Serenity had both felt it. This young man was special. Luther told Serenity about how the man had stayed measured at the violence displayed against him. He stayed cool and collected. He wasn't reactive. They decided to watch him a little more before making their move.

The Sheriff came out of the adjoining room and made her way over to The Collective.

"It's good news," said the Sheriff. "I told the owners that their van had been sold to some Shamans and a Visionary on their Pilgrimage – and they told me, to tell you, that you could keep the van."

"Really?" said Serenity, jumping out of her seat.

"Yes, they're donating it to you, for the cause."

"That's great news Sheriff, thank you very much." said Laquó.

"Sheriff, could Serenity and I have a moment of your time? There's something we'd like to discuss with you."

"Of course, let's go to my office."

After a discussion with the Sheriff, Luther and Serenity then took the young officer into the Sheriff's office to give him the good news. The officer emerged from the room with a large, and surprised, smile on his face. The Collective clapped for him. The Sheriff clapped for him. All the other officers and prisoners followed suit and started clapping, even though they didn't know what they were clapping for. The Sheriff opened a dusty bottle of wheat whiskey from the evidence room and poured a glass for everyone in the jailhouse.

"To officer Zoop Harvey!" said the Sheriff, as she raised her glass.

"To Zoop!" said everyone, raising theirs too.

"That's two finds in a row for me," said Serenity to Colonius.

"You have a rather pleased look on your face." said Colonius.

"I'm happy," said Serenity with a cheeky twinkle in her eye, "and besides, tonight we do celebrate. Luther has popped his Judge cherry!" Serenity gave Luther a big hug. Luther laughed and hugged her back. "Thank you, Serenity. Yes, it is nice to finally be in the pack."

"You've always been in the pack." said Laquó, holding his glass up to Luther's. "You have to be - you're its leader."

Luther smiled and saluted his drink to Laquó.

CHAPTER SIXTEEN
JUDGE 6: Shamus Montgomery of Hermos

Serenity was pleased to be entering Hermos. The Collective had already agreed to visit the Tomalins' Sanctuary towards the end of their stay in the sandy country. Serenity didn't get terribly homesick. Her family where always with her, in her heart and mind, but she was very much looking forward to spending some time with her parents, her old friends and the Tomalins.

The Collective's first stop was Pinnar City. Serenity's father always said it was 'more sand than city.' He was right. Completely surrounded by Hermosian desert, Pinnar City was a tiny, sparkling insect of a city amidst the massive, dusty lake of sand. The city's houses were made of red sandstone and plastered together with black Rokan salt sand. This made an incredibly durable cement-like mixture that could withstand the country's aggressive sandstorms. The Collective had arrived out of season for sandstorms, but in peak trading season. Pinnar City was the Northern epicentre for all trade in the country. Camel sellers, jewellery makers, amulet hunters and importers would flock from far and wide to the bazaar markets in Pinnar City.

The Collective decided to set up camp on the outskirts of the market walls. Many of the merchant travelling colonies camped here and it would be an effective way to mingle and meet locals. It was extremely hot, mostly every day. Luther suffered from dehydration in the first week. His Fraz County lungs were used to a fresh, breezy atmosphere - not this dry, arid air. Colonius was used to it from his time as an amulet hunter here. Serenity grew up in the desert, so the heat was nothing new for her. Shine suffered from food poisoning in the second week. She'd eaten something at a bazaar stall the day before and concluded that this was the cause. In the third week, Laquó had his finger bitten by a basket snake. They're not poisonous, but their bite hurts. By week four, everyone, except Serenity, Colonius and Tremendos had suffered from at least one, if not two, bouts of dehydration and sickness. Pinnar City was a congested place. It was always full of people bustling about. The volume of bodies brought with it a variety of new and exotic germs. Add to that scorching, dehydrating heat from the strong suruplight and a dry, sandy landscape and you had yourself a recipe for illness.

"I think it's time we move on to Protto." said Luther.

The Collective agreed.

Protto was a small town on the upper most Northernly corner of Hermos. It sat niftily between the North-East Hermos coastline and the start of the desert. Many industries and manufacturers set up here and delivered to all parts of Venezeli. The flat planes of Protto made it the ideal base for warehouse construction and development. Items were distributed via the wider roads that went around the desert. The infrastructure was good, albeit slightly neglected. These roads branched out, around the desert, as well as the Hermos coastline and beyond. Distributers used camel riders to deliver smaller items. They used the small sand roads that went into Pinnar City and the deserts' other market towns.

The Collective had set up camp behind a warehouse. You could just about see the Roko Ocean from their base. Colonius had arranged a glass warehouse tour, hoping that The Collective might enjoy some local production knowledge.

Hermos was rich in Prowlonium desert flowers. The flowers were used for all sorts of things, like medicine, food and dyes. They also provided a special tint to Hermosian glass.

The glass warehouse was enormous. It was filled with furnaces, hoppers, tanks, pipes and glass stations. The warehouse had air conditioning, but the temperature was still extremely high. The Collective were excited to learn about glassmaking. Operatives were dotted around the warehouse busily pouring substances from one container into another, mixing things and carrying materials.

Colonius had spotted a man doing some glassblowing. He was mesmerised by it. The man was steady in his craft. He looked focused in the sweltering heat.

Two operatives on the other side of the warehouse started fighting with each other. Colonius watched as the glassblower carefully put down his work, then strode over to the fighting operatives. The man wasn't there long. He resolved the dispute quickly and without fuss. Colonius watched as the man then went back to his work. He headed over to him. The man was about to lift his long metallic pipe-looking object. Colonius quickly put his hand out for a high three.

"My name's Colonius. How are you?"

The man looked confused at first. Then it looked like he understood who the stranger was. He put his glassblower down, smiled warmly and returned Colonius' high three.

"I'm Shamus, nice to meet you. You must be on the tour?"

"Yes! It's fascinating. May I ask what you are working on?"

"We've been commissioned to do some work for the new Supreme Court in Ozro. We'll be making thick glass components for the dome and other decorative items. I'm playing around with ideas for the decorative items." Shamus pointed to his glassblowing apparatus.

Colonius laughed. "For the Supreme Court? Wow, that's really great."

"What's funny?" asked Shamus, genuinely curious.

"Nothing, nothing. Who's your foreman?"

"I am." smiled Shamus.

"In that case, could I have a few moments of your time?

CHAPTER SEVENTEEN
JUDGE 7: Meradin Zykló of Hermos

Shamus had invited The Collective to a ballad ceremony that evening. Shamus was living in a trailer park close to the glassmaking warehouse. Many warehouse workers stayed in trailers during peak season and returned to their families in the off-season. Shamus lived alone. He'd decided to make Protto his home. His colleagues couldn't understand it. Protto was arid and desolate. There was nothing much to do there. It was flat, dry, bare and full of warehouses. It was ugly and boring. Shamus didn't think so. He could find beauty everywhere, no matter what his address. He loved to walk around Protto at night. He would take pictures of the orange-zing streetlights on the empty, geometric bays. He would recognise returning desert foxes looking for scraps. He'd find Prowlonium flowers growing in the most unlikely of places. Prowloniums were tough, they could blossom in places where nothing else could survive. When his colleagues left Protto in the off-season, he did miss their company, but he also appreciated the silence. Protto's horizon was normally a smoky haze, filled with cargo truck fumes and warehouse chimney waste bellowing out at full pelt. In the off-season, a pink tinge would return to the sky. The air quality was better, and you could see the full Hermosian coastline. Shamus loved to surf. In the off-season, he would take his truck, tent and surfboard to Shark Bay, South of Protto, and spend weeks on the water, worshipping the Roko Sea. There were no schools or major communities in Protto. It was a manufacturing town, no one wanted to raise a family here. As an industrial base, it thrived, but when workers returned for start of season, there was a melancholy feel to the air. It was always worst in the first week. Workers' minds were still filled with fresh memories of their loved ones. Upon returning, a realisation kicked in that they would be separated from their families for a large part of the year. After the first month, routine and hard work would replace the melancholy, but when workers got together at the end of the day to relax, they would start to reminisce. This is where Hermosian ballads were born. Protto had a long history of seasonal workers, separated from their families in order to make a decent wage. It was always nice to send zulan home, but the songs captured the sadness of separation. The songs were poignant, touching and incredibly uplifting. They captured a certain Koli - that means all-encompassing energy. Citizens of Universe 5 believe that Koli is the driving force behind birth, life, death and re-birth. It's the matter upon which chance, possibility, destiny, fate and the Dualism Scale also dance their little dance. Venezelians stopped arguing over whose definition was right. They realised, many millennia ago, that they were all right – they'd just spent a long time arguing over whose version was right. There had been fighting and there had been war. Eventually, they agreed to disagree and call it what it was - a force. This was a force that facilitated life. It didn't wholly determine it - free will, choice and consequences were also players at the table – but it was the all-encompassing glue that held it all together.

Shamus and his colleagues had set up seats to make a large oval around their campfire. The surup was low in the sky as everyone gathered around the campfire. Musicians were scattered in between workers and The Collective, so that the music could travel around everyone. Inhabitants of the trailer park were passing around sweet maize-dogs with cherry chilli topping. There was wheat whiskey in abundance.

"This is lovely." said Carmen. She was delighted that they would see the surup-set together. Colonius was sitting next to Serenity. He had been quiet all day. Serenity thought that her friend was in a pensive state after finding Shamus. The entire process of Judge-finding could be quite draining for Shamans. But it wasn't that. Colonius was deep in thought as he listened to the ballad. Was he pining for home? But he was a born adventurer, thought Serenity. A lone wolf, an explorer. What was on his mind tonight?

"Are you ok, Colonius?"

Colonius looked up from his clasped hands. "I was just thinking about my parents."

"Were you tempted to drop in on them when we were in Ozro?" asked Serenity.

"Not really. Where would I start? 'Hi, mother, hi, father. These are my Shaman friends, oh and by the way, I'm a Shaman too."

Serenity laughed. "That would be a direct way to put it to them. Do you miss home?"

"I had to be my own home, Ser. My parents were too concerned with outdoing or impressing their socialite friends. The only way I would have made them happy was to turn into one of them."

"Do you know that, for sure?"

"They registered me for Etonia on my first birthday. They already had my life mapped out for me, just like their parents did for them. I didn't stray to make them angry; I was just listening to a different tune."

"You'd still like their blessing though, wouldn't you?"

"Doesn't every child?"

"So that's what's worrying you?" asked Serenity. "That they wouldn't approve of your life choice?"

Colonius nodded.

"It's easy to follow a pre-determined path or do what others expect of you. It's much harder to carve your own and go against the grain. And saying you 'don't care' about your family's thoughts on it is an easy deception to yourself. You want them to be happy for you, of course you do. You want them to *know* that you are happy. That's only natural." Serenity put her arm around her friend, "You need to find a way Colonius. You need to find a way to tell them who you are. And you need to find a way to assimilate their feelings on it, whatever they are. It doesn't mean you were wrong to follow your instincts."

"You're right. Maybe I'll find the courage…" Colonius hugged his friend. "Hey, when I find my next Judge before you," Colonius teased, "what will that be? Two Judges each and just four more to find? You better be ready to buy me that barrel." Colonius joked. Serenity tickled his ribs, and he let out a deep, hearty laugh.

***

Laquó was transfixed by the surup-set. This part of the day was called evelight. Next would be midlight - a rare and beautiful part of the night where magic could be felt moving through one's veins to the tips of one's hair. Different forming shadows would appear, sometimes comforting, sometimes ominous - it depended on the Koli. And then it would go dark, and the fire light would be born. It was the Duality Scale at play.

Tremendos took a seat next to Laquó. "How are you?" she asked.

"As Shamans, we see so much beauty, but I doubt we can ever really process it all."

"You're feeling reflective, then." smiled Tremendos.

"You could say that, yes." said Laquó, taking a sip of his warm wheat whiskey. "This community of workers, they are very welcoming."

"Yes, they are, and they work so hard for their families."

"I imagine the Supreme Court will look beautiful when it's finished." said Laquó.

"It will. And not just on the outside - on the inside too, with our Judges."

"That's a lovely thought," replied Laquó, "you always say the right thing."

"I just say what I see." replied Tremendos.

The Collective had a wonderful evening, returning to their campsite around midnight. Colonius stayed up until the early hours penning a letter to his parents. He re-wrote it a thousand times over. By morning, he was happy with his message.

The Collective's next stop was Carriénishk, to the South. Carriénishk was known for Prowlonium and textile trade. It was a busy little hub. Colonius decided he would post his letter here, from a Tabac station in the centre of town.

The Collective parked their van on the outskirts of the town's stone walls. Carriénishk looked like an old hamlet or walled-in fortress. The streets were bustling with traders, buyers and local Hermosians. Shine could smell something coming from little pots on the stall stands. She looked closer. They weren't pots, but small vases, and the smoky trail emerging from them smelled like cardamom and brown sugar. Shine saw a Glup Jock for sale on every other stand. She thought it was strange to see Glup Jocks in the desert. They must be over-heating, with their furry little bodies. Glup Jocks were native to Fraz County. They lived in trees and were primarily nocturnal creatures. They liked a cooler clime. Shine was consumed by the market's stimuli and thoughts of those poor Glup Jocks. She hardly felt the tug on her forearm. *What was that?* It was a thief, and they were now around six metres in front of her, running through the crowd. Tremendos had seen them approach and was going to step in, but something told her to hang back. Someone else was on the case. She had to let this one play out.

A woman on a horse appeared into the crowd like a magic trick. All that was missing was the smoke and sound effects. On that horse, was Meradin Zykló, renowned desert transporter and vigilante.

Meradin used her horse, Regina, to chest pump the thief. Regina's blow sent the thief flying. They landed in a large pile of cotton and hessian off-cuts. Meradin stepped off her horse and grabbed the bag from the thief.

"Last warning, Musto." she said. Her tone meant it too. Meradin returned the bag to Shine and asked if she was alright.

"Totally fine, thank you so much for this." Everything happened so quickly that most of The Collective, who were behind Shine, hadn't even noticed what had gone on. Everyone except Tremendos and Laquó, who were now stood next to the kind stranger, ready to introduce themselves.

Shine explained what happened to Carmen and the others. Laquó and Tremendos asked Meradin if they could buy her a drink. Meradin took them to a small Loopsy Hole, a pop-up stand that offered Helados. Helados were a shaved-ice drink, flavoured with Gojine and Prowlonium and served in a large cone.

"Thank you for this," said Meradin, "but there was no need for this kind gesture. A lot of that goes on here, it was a pleasure to help your friend."

"You have good foresight," said Tremendos, "not just when it comes to petty thieves, but in general."

"That's very kind of you." replied Meradin.

"She's a Visionary," said Laquó, "she's good at spotting that stuff."

"One of Laquó's strengths is seeing the integrity in a person. When they are just and fair."

"I believe you have those qualities too, Meradin." said Laquó

"Am I foreseeing that you are going to ask me something...?" said Meradin.

"Indeed, we are." said Tremendos.

The Shaman, Visionary and desert transporter discussed the details. Meradin couldn't give any reason why she should refuse.

"You know," said Laquó, "if we hadn't chosen you for this journey, I think you would have made a great Shaman."

"Healing powers?" said Meradin. "Am not sure I have the concentration for magic."

"I think you do," said Tremendos, "you sport some of the favouring traits."

"Am too nomadic, probably." replied Meradin. "Becoming a Judge will be an honour and a privilege. I promise to devote my life's work to it, you have my word. However, I'll be pleased for my days off, when I can take Regina and ride off into the Ozro evelight. Shamans are on-call all day, every day. It's quite the vocation."

Laquó laughed. "We hope you and Regina will be incredibly happy in Ozro. We'll make sure your base has plenty of outdoor space for her."

Meradin raised her Helado and proposed a toast to the Shaman and the Visionary.

"You guys make a very good team."

Tremendos blushed, an experience she rarely had. You could barely make out the pink smudges on her pale cheekbones. Laquó raised his Helado and said, "Just doing our best."

As Tremendos and Laquó headed back towards the group, Tremendous stopped. She pulled Laquó into a small alleyway behind some robe vendors.

"Laquó," she whispered, "I saw your past."

"What?" asked Laquó.

"That night when we were collecting driftwood. I saw everything."

Laquó's eyes started to tear up. "So, you know why I didn't want to venture into Charno Territory."

"You should have told the others that's where you grew up. No-one would have judged you for that."

"Charno is criminal territory. I worked hard to escape it."

"I know that, and you succeeded. But you still carry your past around with you. If you don't address it, it will continue to cause you great pain."

"You saw…Kaleb?"

Tremendos nodded. "What happened to him, it wasn't your fault Laquó."

Tears were now streaming down Laquó's face. "I was a delinquent, Tremendos. My mother had instructed me to watch my brother. Instead, I went to the quarry with my friends. We stole a car that day. That evening, my parents had to go to the police station for both of us. Only Kaleb was…"

"It wasn't your fault." repeated Tremendos.

"You told your brother to stay at home. Instead, he followed you to the quarry. You weren't to know that he would do that. He slipped, it was an accident."

"I should have stayed with him." Laquó buried his head into Tremendos' shoulder. She stroked his hair. "It wasn't your fault. It was an accident."

Laquó wiped his tears away. "Thank you, Tremendos."

"To journey without being changed is to be a nomad. To change without a journey is to be a chameleon. To journey and be transformed is to be a pilgrim."

"Who said that?" asked Laquó.

"All I know is that his name is Mark Nepo. He lives on a planet in a Universe that I have never heard of and that I can't identify. What I do know, is that Mark hasn't written those words yet, but he will." replied Tremendos.

"How do you know that?" asked Laquó, smiling.

"Because he spoke them out loud, one future night. I glimpsed it, then immediately wrote it down in my little golden notebook."

CHAPTER EIGHTEEN
JUDGE 8: Romins Perpula-Dawn of Hermos

Meradin took it upon herself to give The Collective a tour of the Carriénishk outskirts. She took them to all the famous sightseeing spots and temple ruins. In the evenings, she took them to the best little eateries off the beaten track. Meradin lived and travelled alone, but she knew many families and traders in Hermos. Many of her acquaintances had become extended family. She would often bring them treats and deliveries when passing through. The Collective had a wonderful week. Meradin told them stories of her time as a desert transporter and The Collective were gripped. They had also converted to Helados, their new go-to drink to alleviate the warm, sticky Hermosian desert heat.

The following week, The Collective said their good-byes and thanked Meradin for her hospitality. They headed North-West, for Shark Bay.

Tremendos felt that Hermos had one more Judge for them. She also thought the sea air might be a welcome change from the arid, throat-drying desert. They unanimously decided on Shark Bay, however the van's engine overheated on the way. This delayed their arrival to the coast by another week.

Once they eventually arrived there, The Collective spent two weeks at Shark Bay. It was called Shark Bay because of the high infestation of Desert Sharks, large beasts with many teeth. They didn't like the taste of Venezelians and would often keep to the deeper waters, but a few attacks had been known in past times.

It was a period of re-invigoration for The Collective. They had hired two large beach huts. They spent the evenings eating barbequed fish and dipping their toes in the warm sand. It was a chance to take off their ceremonial robes and let the surup kiss their skin. Tremendos kept her robe on. Visionaries did not surupbathe, but they could swim or paddle with them on. They appreciated the invigorating effects of the Roko Ocean. Its salty particles nourished their hair and skin. It was Luther who benefited most from this part of the Pilgrimage.

Luther spent every day in the Ocean. He felt there was something about this sea water that was healing him. At first, he was fearful of its strong pull. The sea in Venezeli was sensitive to emotion. It was a living, breathing thing. Sometimes it would do its own thing. Other times it would reflect an overriding emotion picked up by people or animals. The sea would toss Luther up, down and around in the surf. Luther learned to hold his breath for a long time. One day, a rip tide almost pulled him down. He was so frightened by this, that he almost didn't step foot in the sea again. But Luther knew he was battling something deep in these waters, something internal that he hadn't addressed. The day after the rip tide incident, he ventured out again. Shine, who was normally scared of the sea, decided to join him. They held hands and went in. Soon, the waves were bouncing them about. Shine started to panic. She looked over at Luther. The fear in his face was tremendous. She decided to put on a brave face and rise above her own fear to help Luther.

"Luther! Look at me," she said, "remember, the sea may have her way with you. She may pull you this way and the next. She may hurt you with the hidden rocks beneath her surface and she may temporarily suffocate you with her might – but, if you relax, if you don't fight it – she will always wash you up to shore. You will bob up from the waves. Let her guide you home."

Shine didn't know where this bravery was coming from. She didn't know where the words were coming from, but out they came. Luther knew she was right. Right then, something shifted inside him. He couldn't live his life fearing being hurt. The waves had taken him through the worst of it, and he was still there. Luther, enlightened, emerged from the water with Shine. He gave her a hug. He felt baptised, re-born.

The Collective had enjoyed their stay at Shark Bay. They had met some wonderful travelling traders and got to know the people who ran the Helados and food stands along the coastline. But there were no future Judges there.

The Collective packed up, got back in their van and headed South, for the Tomalins' Sanctuary. The van smelled of sea salt, sand and surup protective cream. The van got very warm very quickly in the desert. Even though there were windows, the biggest ones were on the driver's and passenger's side. Everyone took their turn to drive, and the passenger seat was shared around too. The Collective were thankful to be travelling down the coastline towards the Tomalins. The cool sea breeze was divine through the front windows.

***

The Tomalins' Sanctuary, in Southern Hermos, was close to the North-West Li border. It was fifteen miles inland of the Hermos coastline. The Sanctuary was based in an area called The Outback. The land in these parts was flat and sparse. Other than the odd Jumulea Tree or manufactured lake, it was primarily dusty. Northern winds would bring hot sand clouds down from the North. Luckily, the Westerly winds from the Roko Ocean and the milder Li climate, across the border, meant that The Outback also experienced cooler temperatures up from the South.

The Sanctuary was a large settlement, surrounded by a barbed wire fence. It had been put there to stop pirates from stealing Tomalins. The settlers had decided to keep it as a reminder and avoid complacency. There were around one hundred families now living with the Tomalins. Despite its flat and bare appearance, The Outback was a harmonious place. The families had developed a community: schools; hospitals; libraries; food outlets, everything one might need. They worked alongside the Tomalins and provided an extra level of care for these endangered creatures. Tomalins were not pets here. This was their environment, their habitat – and the Venezelians were their cohabiters. It was a community harnessed on love, respect, understanding, mutual support and encouragement. Care in the community was at the centre of everything The Sanctuary did. The Tomalins would help the ageing population with odd jobs and company. The Venezelians would provide first-class health and childcare for the Tomalins. Everything worked in harmony.

It had taken a lot for Serenity to leave her home. She missed her parents and the Tomalin community in abundance. It had been thirteen years since she left The Sanctuary. Becoming a Shaman meant little in the way of holiday time, but she did manage one visit home each year. Her mother had retired from nursing. Her father was still a veterinary nurse for the Tomalins.

It was great to be back in The Outback. Serenity knew The Collective would love it here. Colonius knew the place well from his amulet hunting days. Serenity hoped the group might find their ninth Judge here.

The Collective had been at The Sanctuary for two days when Luther spotted Romins Perpula-Dawn for the second time.

Romins' family came to The Sanctuary eight years ago. Romins was fourteen-years old at the time. Now a woman in her twenty-third year, she was happy that her parents and older brother had joined the movement when they did. The Tomalin thefts had stopped some years before their arrival, but many Tomalins still struggled to function after losing so many of their family and friends to the Indigan pirates.

Romins oversaw a first-aid station that annexed the Tomalin hospital base. A Tomalin had come to her station with a cut shin. The gash looked deep, and the Tomalin was in a lot of pain. Luther and Colonius watched as Romins cleaned and dressed the wound.

"This feels like déjà-vu," said Colonius, "it was at a first-aid station that I first saw Serenity." Colonius left Luther and headed back to the group. Luther wanted to stay and watch Romins a while longer.

Romins helpful nature was the type of kindness Luther had often witnessed from those serving on the medical front line. There was something about

Romins' way that particularly intrigued Luther. He had spotted her the day before too, at the butchers. She was helping an elderly Tomalin with her groceries. You could see Romins' eyes light up as she engaged in conversation with the Tomalin. Luther knew that look all too well – it was compassion.

Luther approached Romins at her medical bay. The injured Tomalin had left, and Romins was tidying up some medical supplies.

"Hello." he said.

"Hello." replied Romins. Luther could tell straight away that she was shy. She didn't trust strangers easily.

"I'm Shaman Luther, I'm here with my friends. We're on a Pilgrimage."

***

Romins had taken a lot of convincing. Luther loved her spirit. She reminded him of himself. She had a stubborn streak. She was committed to her current cause. She rejected the Judge's position, stating her work with the Tomalins was too invaluable for the community. Luther told her about his friend, Serenity, who also used to live in the Sanctuary. He told her of everything she had achieved and all the people she had managed to help in her time as a Shaman. Romins fought on, she wasn't easily persuaded. Luther asked her to think about it. He told her to talk to her family. He would come back the following day for her answer.

"Just think of your Tomalin friends," said Luther, "You could be in a position to help their cause on a much grander scale. What you're doing on the front line is very important, and you are great at it, but there comes a time when you need to put your skills and experience to another goal. No matter how much you might try to hide it from people, your compassion got my attention like a lighthouse beaming out into the dark seas. It drew me in to safety, and I knew you could give that guidance to many more. Please," said Luther, "just sleep on it."

Romins didn't sleep at all. Luther's words kept going around in her head. She spoke to her family and friends. In the end, it was her best friend, a Tomalin bear called Massimus, who persuaded her.

"Be our ambassador, Romins," pleaded Massimus.

Tomalins didn't speak, but they signed. Certain noises and movements were also part of their language. It took a while to learn the full breadth of Tomalinian, the Tomalin language, but everyone who lived in The Sanctuary learned soon enough.

"I can't just leave everyone, everything." Signed Romins.

"You can't leave something that lives inside your heart. Please," pleaded Massimus, "do it, for the Sanctuary's future safety."

And with that, Romins decided to join the Supreme Court. She gave Luther her answer the next day. Luther gave her a copy of the Judge's Prophetic Journal, a good luck amulet, all the information she might need and a high three.

"See you soon Romins."

"Take care, Luther, and..."

"Yes?"

"Thank you, for believing in me."

"I know you believe in you too. Never let go of that." Luther said goodbye and joined his friends for the next stage of their journey.

CHAPTER NINETEEN
JUDGE 9: Jakolyn Tempest of Li

It had been thirty-one weeks since The Pilgrimage began. The Collective were now heading South-East, crossing the border into Li. The Sanctuary in Hermos was a straight line away from the North face of the Li mountains. It would take two days for the van to reach the Li mountain foothills. The plan was to drive around the mountain and arrive at the foothill villages on the South face. It was a bright surupy day when The Collective arrived. The mountains were snow-capped, as they always were at this time of year. Carmen took a deep breath in. A thousand memories flooded her nostrils, then her mind. Carmen was from Klerny, in South-East Li, but for now, she felt like she'd come home.

Tremendos was from the Droma Forest in the South-West corner of Li. She knew the North-East mountains well, after many trips here with her study partners from the settlement.

Tremendos asked the group if they wanted to go up the mountain, instead of around it. It was lunar week and the Koli was strong. Tremendos felt a hike up the mountain, in time for midlight, would be the perfect start to their Li journey. They could have a midnight meditation, followed by a Shamanic ceremony. The Collective appreciated having two Li natives available to show them all its beautiful nature trails. They collectively agreed to the hike.

The Collective packed woolen-ware for the summit. Luther packed the group blankets, flasks with gingero tea and some Petri Stones he'd collected earlier that day. Petri Stones were aqua marine-coloured stones found in the Li rivers and waterways. It was a Shamanic tradition to bless Petri Stones on any mountain top. To bless them during lunar would give them healing properties.

It was evelight when The Collective reached the summit. They made a campfire, had some food and started their ceremonies and meditations. When they finished, they could see the most beautiful surup-set on the horizon. It was filled with colours: indigo; orange; crimson; pomegranate; plum; peach; charcoal black and light forest green. Carmen had her dad's notebook of paintings and sketches and her mum's handkerchief on her knee. As she sat on the summit, looking out over her home country, she was hit by a wave of overwhelming gratitude. Gratitude for Shine, for her friends, for the honour of this Pilgrimage, for her work and for everything she had learnt along the way. She also felt sad. With love comes pain. Carmen could feel everything. This meant an intense affinity with other emotions. The pain started in Ozro. Carmen had witnessed much poverty in the administrative capital, Ipa. This posed a sharp contrast with the affluent higher classes who lived in the suburbs. She saw children stealing food, desperate for nourishment. She saw animals caged and maltreated. They were images that she hadn't been able to shake off. Carmen witnessed similar scenes in Pinnar City. Waves of struggling, hungry people. Many without health insurance or options for medical care. For all its bustling commerce and insights from The

Awakening, the reality in Pinnar was a large demographic of people in need.

Shine could tell that Carmen's mind was occupied.

"Are you alright darling?" Shine asked.

Carmen came out of her trance. "Hi, yes, I'm ok. Just been processing our journey so far. Just assimilating everything - the good and the bad."

Shine was aware of Carmen's sensitivities when it came to picking up and feeling emotion.

"I understand. Is there anything I can do? Anything I can get you?"

"Stay with me, for a moment. Just hold my hand."

Shine took Carmen's hand and kissed it. The couple sat in silence for a while. "Aren't Tomalins great?" asked Carmen.

Shine looked at Carmen's face. It was, once again, filled with that joyous sparkle.

"They are." replied Shine.

"I would like to return there one day, volunteer at The Sanctuary for a few weeks. Perhaps revisit Ipa and Pinnar City, help the homeless and vulnerable."

"We can do that, darling."

"Thank you. I'd like that."

After suruprise, The Collective came down the other side of the mountain. Prior to the climb, Luther had parked the van on the Southern foothills, in anticipation of their descent. The people who lived at the foothills were friendly and hard-working. They were mostly ranch owners, sheep herders and wheat pickers. Their humility and persistence warmed Carmen's heart. It was an ethos she had grown up with. The Collective didn't meet anyone of judiciary interest in the villages, so they moved on. Next on the itinerary were the South-Western forests of Li.

Li was a mystical place. If Fraz County was known for magic and spirituality, Li was known for mysticism, psychic phenomena and mythical creatures. Granite workers often told fables about forest fairies when round the campfire. Fisher people on the coast spoke of mermaids who watched over their boats. The foothills were famous for stories about wandering centaurs. Carmen had never witnessed any of these things, but it didn't mean that she didn't believe in them. Tremendos, on the other hand, studied these creatures as part of her daily curriculum. When people from Li sang country songs, they would often reference these creatures. To the people of Li, these creatures were real, not mythical. Li was a place shrouded in the mystical, and nowhere more so than the inland settlement of Droma Forest.

Tremendos would have loved to bring the Shamans into the heart of her settlement. She wanted them to meet her teachers and elders. However, due to an ancient law, no-one, other than approved Visionaries, could enter the settlement. Visionary practices were ancient and shrouded in secrecy.

Out of respect, The Collective parked their van around five miles from the Droma Forest. Tremendos looked serene in these forests, thought Laquó. Something ancient and knowing exuded from her blue-green petroleum eyes. Recently, Laquó had been experiencing a deep feeling in his chest every time Tremendos looked his way. It felt warm and familiar. It felt safe. It felt like home. Laquó watched as Tremendos spoke to some forest animals. She was telling them not to be afraid, that

The Collective were her friends. Laquó didn't realise how beautiful Tremendos was, until now. Tonight, he saw her in a different light.

The Collective sat around the campfire, enjoying the crisp, fresh forest air, a welcome difference from the stifling Hermos heat. Laquó noticed Tremendos' long flowing hair. Why had he never noticed how silky and mesmerizingly metallic it looked? Laquó watched how it flowed onto her lap. Her gentle hands crossed neatly on her lap. She had her eyes closed. Was she enjoying the glow from the fire's flames behind her eyelids? Was her mind a million galaxies away? Did she ever think of him? Laquó remembered her touch that night at the Cardinal Lake base in Ozro. It had sent a soothing warm ripple across his skin. He had been craving that touch again. Just at that, Tremendos opened her eyes and looked across the campfire straight at Laquó. Laquó blushed, hoping she wouldn't notice. He hoped she would think it was the fire's warmth that burned his cheeks. Tremendos smiled at Laquó, and his heart melted further.

***

A week after the forest search, The Collective carried on South-East, to the Li coastline and the main granite quarries. The Shamans took the opportunity for a swim in one of the quarries. Tremendos and Laquó sat it out.

"I thought about what you said," said Laquó, "about Kaleb."

Tremendos had removed her boots and was airing her feet in the surup. She had never exposed her feet to anyone before, but with Laquó, she felt free and unrestricted.

"I made my peace with him that night, at the summit. I made peace with myself. I embraced the lunar's energies and let the guilt assimilate. I didn't hide it or dig it away somewhere. I confronted it. I embraced it. I learned to find a place inside me where it could rest. I understood that it's a part of my life, so I can't unimagine it. I just had to find a way to stop it from consuming everything good in my life."

"That is wonderful, Laquó." said Tremendos. She placed her hand on his.

Laquó's chest felts like liquid heat. "You don't need to be a mind reader to know how I feel about you Tremendos."

Tremendos smiled.

"But I'm going to say it out loud anyway…"

"Wait…" said Tremendos.

"What is it?" asked Laquó.

"I've been having some very intense visions today. Whether it's being so close to home, or another sign, or something significant – I'm not sure. But I feel really drained right now, and I want to be fully present when you say what you're going to say."

"You want my amulet?"

"Yes please, just for a second."

Laquó pulled out a bone amulet. It was a very large Desert Shark tooth.

"There's a long story behind this one," said Laquó, "but it's been enchanted with a strength charm."

"Perfect! Just what I need." replied Tremendos.

She held the amulet in her hand for a few seconds.

Laquó could see rosy colour flush back into her gorgeous cheekbones.

"Thank you." said Tremendos. "You were saying?"

"I love you."

"I love you too."

Laquó moved a strand of Tremendos' soft, flowing hair away from her face. He gently kisses her lips.

"You see me," said Laquó, "and not just because you're a Visionary."

Tremendos smiled.

"You see me like no one else can, or ever has," he continued, "I promise to always watch out for you, in all dimensions, for all time."

"As will I." said Tremendos.

***

The Collective met quarry workers from all parts of Li. They sang together, told stories around the fire and tried some of the best, home-grown Li wheat whiskey they had ever tasted. Even Carmen and Tremendos didn't remember it tasting so good. The quarries were close to the coast, but The Collective would not be continuing East, along the coast. Instead, they had decided to snake up and down the country. They would continue in a North-Easterly direction through the woodcutter woods. This would spit them out in Deep Country, the Grand Ole Colony in the North.

The Grand Ole Colony was right bang in the centre of North Li, close to the Zaattan border. It was famous for producing some of the best country singers in all Venezeli. Its hub was the Merry Weathers Roundhouse, one of the largest country music venues in all of Venezeli.

There was a music festival on at the moment. Carmen was desperate to take The Collective there for some sound nourishment of the soul. The Roundhouse was packed to the rafters. Visitors from everywhere would come for their musical fix. If Hermos was home of the melancholy ballad, The Grand Ole Colony was home to the best uplifting country music.

The Collective were staying in a motel in the centre of the Grand Ole Colony. This was normally impossible during festival time, but one of Carmen's oldest friends was a manager at the Roundhouse. The venue would always hold some extra accommodation back for special guests and musicians.

The Roundhouse was huge. It sounded small, but it was a top-class arena with an old-style country feel. The auditorium sat in the centre of the Roundhouse and looked like a massive beehive. Balconies looped round and round to a seemingly infinite point at the very top.

There were musicians everywhere. The bar tops were flowing with wheat whiskey. An array of drinks and snacks adorned every barrel table. The Collective couldn't believe their eyes.

The night's entertainment began. The Collective laughed and cried together. They heard musicians play their songs with an array of weird and wonderful instruments.

After the interval, the first act on was a musician called Jakolyn Tempest.

"I've heard good things about this artist." Carmen told Shine as they took their seats again in the beehive auditorium.

The lights dimmed. A red filter highlighted half the stage. Jakolyn walked out and sat down on a chair, centre stage. It was just her, a microphone and her Killerno. She started to sing. Within seconds, Carmen was crying. She looked over the rest of her group. Luther was in floods of tears and, to Carmen's surprise, even Serenity was crying. Carmen had never seen that kind of vulnerability from Serenity before. She was the joker, the light-hearted entertainer of the group. The others were mesmerised, gripped by Jakolyn's every word, but it was just herself, Luther and Serenity who seemed transformed by the performance. And why wouldn't they be, thought Carmen. Jakolyn's lyrics and music went together in such a way that it spoke straight to the heart. Carmen looked down at her arms. She had goosebumps.

The rest of the evening was electrifying. Bands got the entire auditorium to their feet. Tremendos had never been to the Colony. She was moved by its Koli. There was a profound sense of unity amongst the patrons and musicians who had come together at the Roundhouse.

At the end of the show, Luther asked Carmen if she might be able to introduce him to Jakolyn.

"Oh wow!" said Carmen, "did you sense it too?"

Luther blushed.

"Oh," laughed Carmen, "I thought you'd sensed her Judge potential!"

"Oh no," laughed Luther, "I hadn't. I did feel something though. She moved me, in ways that I haven't felt for a long time."

"Wait here," said Carmen, "let me speak to my friend and see if she can get us into the musician's after-party in the green room."

Carmen pulled it off. She got all seven of them into the after-party.

The green room was a large hexagonal shaped room with floor-to-ceiling windows. Musicians were singing, laughing and drinking the evening away. Luther spotted Jakolyn talking to two women by the bar.

"Carmen, she's over there."

"Thanks Luther. I'll go talk to her first, see if my senses were right. If I think she's the one, I'll introduce you before going into the whole 'you are the chosen one' speech – don't want to burst your bubble by blowing her mind first." winked Carmen.

"I appreciate that." said Luther.

Carmen's instincts were right. Jakolyn was an individual driven by pure unconditional love. They spoke for around forty minutes. Carmen asked Jakolyn about her origins, her family and her music. The conversation flowed easily, and Carmen could have spoken to her all night. She saw Luther out of the corner of her eye. He had been waiting patiently. He had a wheat whiskey in his hand and looked as nervous as a Glup Jock.

"Jakolyn, I'd like to introduce you to a friend of mine, if I may?"

"Yes, of course." replied Jakolyn.

It was love at first sight. Love was Carmen's department anyway, but she was sure even a piece of Jorkey stone from the depths of the Roko Ocean could have seen the sparks fly between Jakolyn and Luther. Carmen left them alone to talk.

Serenity was on a giant beanbag, lost in her own thoughts. The enormous beanbag looked like it might envelop her at any minute. Carmen approached her.

"Hey Serenity, can I join you?"

"Sure." Serenity budged up, careful not to disappear into the beanbag entirely. Carmen sat on the opposite end. "I couldn't help but notice…Jakolyn's performance really touched you, didn't it?"

Serenity smiled. "Now don't get all gooey on me Carmen," she quipped, "but yes, it did ignite a realisation."

"May I ask what that was?"

"You know, since I can remember, I've always tried to live in the present. Growing up in The Sanctuary, there was always lots going on. There was love and pain and all the rest, but I saw my place as the one who could lift the mood, you know?"

Carmen nodded.

"I've always been dedicated to my work, whatever that was. First, The Sanctuary and now Shamanism, and I wouldn't change that for the world – this is my path."

"But...?" intervened Carmen.

"But...I'm lonely, Carmen. Like, I didn't even realise I was."

"You mean, romantically?"

"Yes. I've never really allowed myself the time or space to engage in that kind of relationship with anyone. When I heard Jakolyn's song, I felt like someone had punched me in the heart. Isn't that crazy, how a song can do that?"

"It's powerful stuff. Music is someone pouring their thoughts and emotions out for all to see. If you can relate to that, it's one more person to identify with. Sometimes it's not even the lyrics, it's the music itself that speaks to you."

"For me, I think it was a mixture of both. It was like a wake-up call. I've been afraid, Carmen. I've been so afraid to open myself up like that. Isn't that strange?"

"Not really. It is scary. Love wouldn't be love if it were a simple thing."

"I'm going to be more present in my own love story," said Serenity, "and I think it has to start with me. I need to take some time to ask myself some questions. What do I want? What can I give? What do I want to give and how do I plan to give it? How do I plan to love another? What love do I feel I deserve? I need to take care of myself first. I might have the courage to put myself out there again."

"That sounds terrific, and definitely, do that work. Get comfortable too, don't worry about the timeline on it. Those things will take care of themselves. Make a commitment to yourself, and to keeping your eyes and ears open, my lovely. Some opportunities may not be the right ones, but they could help you learn something that you need to know. I don't need to explain that to you, you're a Shaman, you know how symbolism works. It's not too different with love. When you have shed your insecurities and fears, be vigilant. The rest will come. And when it does, be brave. Be proactive. Have courage. Dive in if you must. Get hurt if you must. If no chances come up, and you're quite content that way, then so be it - that's good also. You don't need to force anything upon yourself. It's great to be content on one's own, in fact, it's better that way. You're in a position of not needing anyone and just enjoying love, family and community in all its forms. But if something does present itself, you see it and you want it – well, if you don't take a chance in that scenario, then you might just miss out on a great addition to your life."

"Thank you, Carmen."

Carmen gave Serenity a hug and then made her way over to Shine, who was out on the balcony looking at the shadows dancing during midlight.

"Carmen! My love."

Shine grabbed Carmen by the waist and pulled her in tight. She kissed her like she hadn't seen her in a hundred years.

"Marry me." said Carmen.

"What?" said Shine.

"Be my wife." Carmen's heart was beating hard. Had she asked too soon? Would she scare Shine away?

Shine was quiet. She pulled away from Carmen and looked out at the horizon.

"What's wrong?" asked Carmen, "Am I being too hasty?"

"It's not that," said Shine, crying.

"What is it my love?"

"It's just that, I've been waiting all day to ask you that very same question." Shine got down on one knee and pulled a small box out of her pocket. She opened it. Tears flooded her face as she presented Carmen with a ring. It was an oval-shaped glass stone, fused with yellow Prowlonium on a white gold band.

"I bought it, in Carriénishk," said Shine, "I almost fainted when that thief stole my bag. It had the ring inside. I'd only bought it an hour earlier."

Carmen gasped, putting her hands to her mouth.

"So," asked Shine, "do you?"

"I do!" yelled Carmen, "I most definitely do." Carmen and Shine embraced. The midlight shadows in the Grand Ole Colony were tinged with stars and started dancing with joy.

CHAPTER TWENTY
JUDGE 10: Danny Dove of Li

Jakolyn Tempest had accepted Carmen's offer to become a Judge. She was shocked and surprised, but she accepted immediately. The next day, The Collective decided to head directly South, to Klerny.

Klerny was a fishing and mining town in Southern Li, close to the Fraz County peninsula and coastline. It was where Carmen was born and raised. Carmen's mother had retired and was living in a community hub for ex-fishing families. She had always been quite a solitary person, but she loved the company at the hub. She kept active and liked to knit. Carmen tried to visit at least twice a year, but it could be difficult at times. The Shamanic lifestyle was a busy one, so Carmen made sure to make her holidays count. She would take her mother down to the sea-front and they would bird-spot together. Carmen was so excited to tell her mother the news of her engagement. She often spoke to her mother about Shine. She'd never confessed her true feelings for Shine, but her mother already knew, as mothers do. Every time Carmen talked about Shine, her eyes would light up. The creases in her dimples would deepen and her posture would straighten, like she was full of electricity and hope.

It had taken The Collective a full week to travel South cross-country to Klerny. Even with the van, this was a long journey. They were going from the very North to the very South. They had stopped at motels along the way. There were no majorly inhabited places on this stretch between the Grand Ole Colony and Klerny. There were hills, rivers, moors and small forests, but few communities.

Carmen had picked up a ring for Shine in a small mining outpost. It was a resin mix of Li granite and Jorkey stone on a white gold band, two of the most valuable stones in all of Venezeli. Jorkey was a place of mystery, an old underwater city in the depths of the Roko Ocean off the coast of Li, near the Dorma Forest. Visionaries hailed it as a place of great importance, a lost city with mermaids and hidden treasure. Few had seen the mermaids with their own eyes, and no one had ever found any treasure, but they did discover Jorkey stone. Jorkey stone was an incredibly strong, durable stone, said to have magical properties. There was a distillery in the Li hills that made Jorkey whiskey, a strong and potent drink not for the light-hearted. It was born in the years when wheat whiskey was illegal. It is said that the makers press their whiskey through some tightly packed pebbles from the Jorkey ruins. This filtration process is what gives it its indistinguishable taste. Once revoked, the Jorkey whiskey was still popular in some circles, even though it was renowned for blowing one's head off.

Shine loved her engagement ring, and The Collective had spent a whole week celebrating the news.

Once in Klerny, The Collective set up camp on the beach. The weather was perfect, warm in the day and cool in the evening, never too hot or too cold.

Tremendos would sit and watch the sea for hours. From her normal base in the Dorma Forest, she never ventured this far East. The Li coastline wasn't far from where she lived, but any days out were restricted to the Li mountains in the North-West. She welcomed seeing new parts of her home country. There was something about Klerny that resonated within her. She couldn't put her finger on it yet, but she had that feeling again.

The Collective spent three weeks in Klerny. They spent time with Carmen's mother at the hub and got to know the fisher people at the harbour. They ventured to the local quarries and mines and eat a lot of creamy ice-cream cones.

Luther was sitting on a jetty at the harbour's edge. He was writing his fifth letter to Jakolyn. She was a keen letter-writer too. The pair had been communicating like this since Luther left the Grand Ole Colony. Luther knew she was the one. He couldn't wait to introduce her to his parents back in Fraz County. Luther had been thinking a lot about his future. The night he met Jakolyn, his life felt different, like a new path had appeared. He was excited about her joining the Supreme Court and was considering asking her to move in together in Ipa. He'd never met anyone he felt he could be that open with. No games, no second guessing and no fear about coming on too strong. They were both on the same page. They wanted each other. Given that Luther was still on the Pilgrimage, they decided to continue their courtship one letter at a time, for now.

Colonius had taken up fly fishing and he was getting good at it. Serenity was giving it a go but kept accidentally catching flounder plants. She felt more than a little guilty about it.

Flounder plants were fish, native to planet Indigo. When commercial space travel took off, there were many incidents of animal cross breeding and relocation. Indigan pirates were constantly trying to hustle Venezelian species back to their planet. Tourists would bring over samples of theirs. Not all organisms took well to the differing atmospheres and ecosystems. The flounder plant fish ended up thriving on Venezeli. They had blue-green jelly skin. They looked like baby octopi with faces. They had no teeth and a button nose. They looked like cartoon fish with a person's face. It sounded terrifying, but they were actually extremely cute. They liked to play with people. They could spit water at a range of up to fifteen metres. People didn't eat flounder plants - and it wasn't just because it had a person-looking face. They tasted disgusting. Somebody once said that eating a flounder plant tasted like eating pen ink mixed with battery acid.

Tremendos was staring out to sea, lost in the depths of her own thoughts. Laquó came to sit beside her, he had two ice-cream cones in hand.

"This is such a beautiful country." he said, offering her an ice-cream cone.

She smiled and accepted it. Tremendos had developed a new love for Klerny's ice cream.

"It really is. We have a beautiful planet."

"Are you looking forward to our trip to Jenar?" asked Laquó, taking a lick of his cone.

"I am," replied Tremendos, "but I can't shake the feeling that we still have a Judge here. It's like he's right in front of me, but for some reason, I can't see him."

"It's a him?" enquired Laquó, impressed by Tremendos' foresight. If Tremendos sensed it was a man, he had no doubt it would be.

"Is there anywhere we haven't looked?" asked Laquó.

Tremendos shot to her feet like she'd just had an electrical charge bolted into her body.

"The water!" exclaimed Tremendos, "We haven't tried the water! Oh, thank you Laquó! I'll be right back." Tremendos gave Laquó a great big kiss and ran off down the pier, almost dropping her ice cream on the way.

Tremendos' epiphany was to hire a boat from a local skipper. She secured The Oracle, a large croaha fishing boat, designed for a crew of up to ten people. The next day, The Collective were on the waters.

Colonius was not a huge fan of the sea. He was fine on terra firma, but the Ocean had always scared him. He was aware of its powers. It had the ability to make him feel incredibly seasick.

Tremendos felt guilty. "I'm so sorry, Colonius. If my instincts are right, we shouldn't be out here too long." She passed him a cup of water and headed back to the controls where Luther was steering the boat. Colonius perched over the side of the boat, not sure if he was going to be sick. As he leaned over, a mermaid came up to the surface. She had long fluorescent green hair and sparkling green eyes. She smiled directly at him. Colonius could not believe his eyes. He went to speak, to alert the others, but he had lost his voice. She swam alongside the boat for a few minutes and then disappeared underneath.

"Serenity!" yelled Colonius, "You're never going to believe what I just saw."

***

The waters were moderate for the first few days. The Collective met a few fishing boats in the shallower waters, but no sign of the man Tremendos was looking for. As they ventured into deeper waters, the waves became choppier. Serenity was loving it, the ups and downs, the power of the sea beneath their feet. They passed lobster boats and large croaha fish boats, but still no Judge.

The Collective had been at sea for four weeks. Colonius had overcome his seasickness and was thoroughly enjoying fishing off the deck every day. Luther had become a master boat captain, something he didn't know he could do a month before. Laquó had learned how to build nets and took charge of catching their daily food. Shine was on her two-hundredth Lojo Doll and had hand-stitched waterproof ponchos for everyone in the group. She had also overcome her fear of the sea. Carmen fell in love with the dawn and the surup-set every day and every night. She had never witnessed the surup and lunar this way before. The eerie quiet of the open sea became a soothing and welcomed thing. This month-long meditation was exactly what The Collective needed. Everyone, except for Laquó, had started to lose faith that they would find anyone out here. They hadn't seen another boat or person for two weeks now, but they didn't complain or challenge Tremendos. They made good of this rest bite. They tried to connect with themselves and each other. It was nice to take a break from travelling and walking so much. They did daily exercise together every morning after dawn meditation. They used the time to process all that had been, all that was and all that could be. They laughed, they eat, they drank and told stories. The kept each other's protective surup cream topped up. They talked and sat in silence. They watched the odd Desert Shark pop its head up. Colonius, nor anyone in The Collective, ever saw another mermaid. Serenity took charge of the evening Zoto games. Instead of zulan, the group gambled with seashells. The Oracle was a great boat. She was in good condition and did well in these deeper waters. Carmen had started to draw again. She felt close to her father. She couldn't believe it had been eight years since he passed. She took inspiration from images in her head, the harbour in Klerny and her tent by the sea in Fraz County. She also drew things in her immediate surroundings: the surup-sets; the sea at dawnlight, Shine as she slept – she never felt she could ever quite capture their beauty. Carmen's father used to have that same feeling when he painted. Carmen was looking out at the infinite horizon. Li's coastline had been out of sight for weeks. Suddenly, she saw, what looked like, a tiny triangle appear on the horizon. She blinked, unsure if it was a hallucination from too much time under the strong surup rays. It was still there and getting bigger.

"Tremendos! Tremendos!" shouted Carmen, almost causing Colonius to tip over the boat with his fishing rod.

"There's another boat!"

Tremendos and Luther sailed towards the stranger's boat. It was a small, white, single sailboat. Its owner was a tall man with chin-length sandy-blonde hair and freckles. Tremendos had found him – it was Danny Dove.

***

Danny Dove was a nomadic sailor with no fixed address. He'd been sailing the Roko Seas alone since he was a teenager. His family were a sea-borne family. Danny was born on a lobster boat. When

Danny turned sixteen, his sister, Prentice, died in a tragic fishing accident. She loved night fishing, but her parents and brothers would never allow her to do it alone. One night, rather than waking up her brothers whom she thought looked so peaceful, Prentice went to the back of the boat and pulled out her fishing gear. Something went wrong. She was pulled overboard and down into the deep Li waters. By the time her family awoke the next day there was no sign of her. The family searched for weeks. Local enforcement officers helped with the search, but it was to no avail - her body was never recovered. The family decided to buy a ranch at the foothills of the Li mountains. They vowed never to set foot on a boat again. Danny didn't. He carried on sailing. He sailed and sailed and sailed. No-one in his family could talk him into coming home. He said the sea was his home. He spent years sailing around the continent's circumference. He stopped only to stock up on fuel and food.

    Tremendos invited Danny to come onto The Oracle. He refused. She asked permission to come onto his boat. He accepted but said only she could come on board.

    Tremendos took Danny's hand when embarking onto his boat. Within a second, she knew his story. She felt his pain for his lost sister. Tremendos also felt the one thing she'd been searching for this entire trip – hope. This man was filled with it. He understood his family's standpoint. He didn't think they had given up. He knew they had made their peace with Prentice's death. It was different for Danny. He had to live by the beat of his own drum. A voice in his head said, 'stay on the water.' He didn't know why, but he couldn't stop sailing. Leaving the ocean would mean to stop listening to his inner instinct. It was this inner compass that convinced Tremendos he was their last Venezeli Judge. She knew it but would bide her time before approaching him about it. Danny had unfinished business. Tremendos was sure she could help.

As a life-long sailor, Danny had amazing foresight. He had to be able to read the weather, hour to hour. It was the difference between another day on the water or one spent crashed into a rocky coastal cliff. Tremendos knew he loved the sea, but she also knew that he had stayed out there for a purpose that he wasn't entirely sure of. Tremendos couldn't tell him where his sister was, she didn't know. She couldn't see it just by touching him, but she had an idea.

Tremendos asked Danny if he could take her to their old boat, the one the family used to sail on. Danny was horrified by this at first, but when Tremendos explained her plan, Danny changed his mind. His family boat, The Endurance, was in a lock-up near the Klerny harbour. As Tremendos and Danny made their way to the lock-up, The Collective went for burgers at one of the diners on the harbour's seafront. They'd all had their fill of seafood.

On entering the lock-up, Tremendos could sense Danny's pain.

"I'm sorry, Danny. I knew this wouldn't be easy."

"It's ok," replied Danny, "let's do this."

Tremendos pulled out a small hessian pouch from her shoulder bag. Inside, were seven amulets.

"What are those?" enquired Danny.

"A little help from my friends." replied Tremendos. "I'm going to need all the strength I can muster for this. No promises, ok?"

"I understand," replied Danny, "I appreciate that you are trying this."

"Whatever happens," said Tremendos, "if you see a change in me, please, whatever you do, do not interrupt this. I will be fine; I know when to stop."

Danny nodded and showed Tremendos to the back of The Endurance, the spot where Prentice had spent her last living moments.

Tremendos poured the various amulets into her left hand. She placed her right hand on the back of the boat. She saw it straight away. It was Prentice's face. She looked peaceful, like in a deep sleep. *Focus, Tremendos, focus.*

Tremendos felt beads of sweat rolling down her back. As she honed in on Prentice's face, she tried to hang on to that vision and slowly spread it out. Tremendos could see ruins, seaweed and flounder plants. Tremendos felt her blood pressure lower. A chill started to appear across her body, her lips start to discolour. *Focus, don't let go.*

She got it. She saw the wider picture. Prentice was lying at the bottom of the Jorkey ruins. Mermaids had found her many miles from where the boat had been. Unsure of her origins, the mermaids brought her down to the ruins. They gave her a full mermaid's funeral. They sang sea enchantments, covered her in deep sea flowers and left her to rest in peace. Tremendos could see the beautiful young woman surrounded by mermaids. The contours of the woman started to disappear. In her place, Tremendos could see a skeleton, still covered in fresh deep-sea flowers. The mermaids tended to her grave regularly. Prentice had never been left alone.

"Tremendos! Tremendos! Can you hear me?" It was Danny. He was kneeling next to Tremendos, who had collapsed on the floor.

"I'm fine." said Tremendos, gasping for breath.

"You are freezing cold." said Danny, trying to help Tremendos back to her feet.

Tremendos held on to the back of the boat and steadied herself.

"I know where she is, Danny. Let us help you get your sister, and let's take her home."

CHAPTER TWENTY-ONE
JUDGE 11: Duandarin Krespos of planet Jenar

The Dove family had asked The Collective to carry out Prentice's ceremony. It was a beautiful morning on the foothills of the Li mountains. Luther led Prentice's ceremony in the Dove's private ranch grounds. They found a perfect resting place for Prentice in the paddock next to the river. Danny felt relieved that his sister was reunited with them. He took a deep breath. It felt like the first proper breath he'd taken in eleven years.

"Thank you, Tremendos." said Danny.

Tremendos was looking up at the Li mountains. The surup was beaming beautiful light onto its snow-capped peaks.

"You know, we meditated up there not too long ago. When I was up there, I had a feeling we'd be back here."

"Without your powers, we would never have found my sister."

"Without you, none of us would be standing here again. You found her, Danny. Your reluctance to leave the water is what led us here. You were steadfast, you are steadfast. You were just waiting for us to find you."

"Thank you for staying on the water," said Danny.

"I was just following your lead." replied Tremendos. "Listen, Danny, we have to leave today, for Fraz County. We need to report back to our leader tomorrow and then we get a few days off before we set off for Jenar. I know it's the day of Prentice's funeral and I don't want to put too much pressure on you...but I need to ask you something, and I would like your answer in one week's time. I will send a Visionary friend of mine to your home and you can tell them your decision."

Tremendos knew that Danny didn't have a legitimate reason to refuse the offer. However, if Danny refused, this was an exception Tremendos was willing to make. She hoped he would listen to his internal voice. She was sure he would accept. But if it didn't, she would know it wasn't to be.

***

The week before The Collective flew to Jenar had been a busy one. The group filed an in-depth report on all their Judges. They had fed back bits and pieces of information over the last year so that operational teams in Fraz County and Ipa could start to reach out. Information was sent to the Judges at monthly intervals. The operatives also collected information such as current living arrangements and gown sizes.

The in-depth feedback was specific. It included various kinds of analytical data and the Shamans shared feedback on the Pilgrimage as a whole. This process took around three days.

Cressida was delighted to see The Collective again. She was concerned that the last Judge hadn't yet given them a definitive answer, but she trusted Tremendos. She agreed that if Danny refused, they would continue the Pilgrimage after their return from Jenar. There was never a set date for the Koli Ceremony. The Ceremony always depended on when The Collective finished their journey in full.

Cressida gave The Collective four days off before they had to assemble in Ipa for de-briefing and departure to planet Jenar.

Cressida had been busy setting up the Herratta cavern for the Laying Down ceremony. The Laying Down ceremony was a process where The Collective would take the original Prophetic Journals, on papyrus, and hide them in a special nook in the cavern. They would place an enchantment on the Journals, protecting them from removal or touch, until the day of the next First Contact, where they would be removed and celebrated no matter which country made First Contact.

During the mini-break, Colonius went fly fishing on the Fraz County shoreline. He still hadn't had a response from his parents since sending his letter from Carriénishk in Hermos. He was hoping for something on his cabin doormat, back in Fraz, but he came home to nothing but advertisements and zulan-off coupons. Disheartened, he took his fishing gear and a tent and disappeared off to the coast. Laquó and Tremendos returned to his woodcutter's hut at the edge of the forest. It was four days of bliss for them. They slept in and drank gingero tea on Laquó's porch. Tremendos would read to Laquó in the evenings by chiandle light. She tried to teach him how to listen and talk to plants. They were happy and felt grounded with each other. On the fourth day, Tremendos checked in with her friend, Sofias, from Dorma Forest. She was anxious to hear Danny's answer.

"He said 'Count me in'" reported Sofias over the phone, "and that was before I'd even stepped inside his front door!"

Tremendos was delighted. She knew he was the right choice for their tenth Judge. Some added good news was that they wouldn't have to re-start their search after their return from Jenar.

On her first day off, Serenity went straight to Christian's Bar. This time, her aim wasn't to try and drink locals under the table or beat bikers at Zoto. This time, Serenity was there to see Christian. She straightened up her best black jumpsuit with black shoulder cardigan and bravely stepped into Christian's bar. *Can I win his heart?* She concluded this would be better than any firecracker whiskey prize. Serenity didn't know it, but Christian had been in love with her for a long time. He had missed her and was delighted to see her walk back through his door. They sat at the bar, talked, drank, sang and opened their hearts to one another.

Shine and Carmen spent two days at Carmen's tent by the sea and two days at Shine's cottage. They learned about each other's favourite things. Carmen listened with eager interest as Shine showed her her Lojo work desk. Shine smiled as Carmen took her on a seashell hunt along the beach periphery, where the sand met the woods.

Luther went to see his parents. He cooked for them and told them all about his journey, including the part where he fell in love with Jakolyn Tempest. He promised he would introduce them to her as soon as possible. Luther's mother handed him one of her rings.

"You've found her," said Madelina, "just like your father found me at that conference."

"I always thought it was you who stalked me?" joked Henry Jung, "I was just minding my own business at the water cooler when this incredibly beautiful young woman started talking to me."

Madelina smiled and rolled her eyes.

"Take it, Luther. I know you want this woman in your life."

Luther took the ring and kissed his mother's forehead.

Happiness and joy burst from his heart. And then, sadness. He knew he would be leaving Fraz County and moving to Ipa to live with Jakolyn there. As a qualified Shaman, Luther could live and set up his practice anywhere in Venezeli. Most Shamans chose to reside in Fraz County because of its Shamanic birthplace. Large Shamanic communities were already in place there. But Luther knew that Jakolyn had no choice. She would have to live in Ipa. Supreme Court obligations meant long days in court and attendance at short notice. Luther took his parents' hands in his.

"I love you. Thank you for everything you've ever taught me, done for me and supported me with. I appreciate every bit of guidance and love you've given me and that you continue to give me."

"We're your parents. We brought you into this world to do that very thing. It's the singular most important thing we've ever done together. We love you, Luther. It's a new chapter for you, go live it, with all the love in your heart."

***

It took The Collective three days of space travel to arrive at Jenar. Space travel had been going for some time in Universe 5, but it was expensive. Only wealthy tourists could afford the trip. The ideal was that one day all people of all backgrounds could afford to visit their reachable neighbouring planets, in their galaxy. As it stood, the only way to visit them for free was through the study and practice of dream travel. It was being taught in all schools and community colleges. There were Scatternet videos on the subject so you could teach yourself at home. Most people started this process after First Contact. Jimus Krakovia taught everyone how to do it.

Venezelian's space travel routes were restricted to Indigo, Jenar, Crystalis and Hydros.

Jenar had presented itself from Cressida's mirror bowl a week before The Collective set off on the Pilgrimage. Jimus Krakovia's instructions had been clear: whatever planet appeared in the mirror bowl would have to comply with the operational requirements.

Lead Shamans would have to choose five potential candidates for their competing planet's consideration. They would have the time it takes The Collective to find their ten judges. These candidates would be vetted by the Administration and a panel interview would be arranged in that country's capital. The Collective would have to travel to Jenar's capital, Reesa, for this process.

Cressida had been asked to provide five candidates from Venezeli for planet Crystalis. She was pleased with that. Indigo was notorious for shady dealings, entrepreneurial pirates and underhanded tactics - she would have been upset if she had to send anyone from Venezeli to Indigo.

Venezeli's ambassador would come from Jenar. Reesa looked a lot like Ipa, other than the green sky and warmer climate.

After the panel interview, The Collective voted anonymously for their country's ambassador in the Supreme Court. It was seven votes clear for Duandarin Krespos.

Duandarin was a nurse at Reesa Hospital. Luther and Laquó had an instinctive feeling about him at first sight, even before the candidates made their presentations to The Collective.

By the end of the process, they were even more convinced, as was the rest of The Collective.

Duandarin was kind, compassionate, virtuous, brave and believed in true justice. He was passionate about saving lives. He provided top quality care at the Hospital and was regarded by those who knew him as grounded, selfless and a good judge of character. It was the easiest selection The Collective had made yet.

"Seven votes clear," said Serenity, "that's incredible."

"We must have tuned into each other more than we thought," replied Colonius.

Luther gave Duandarin his enchanted amulet as they stepped onto the jet heading back to Venezeli. It had been hard for Duandarin to say goodbye to his friends and family, but he was honoured at the opportunity and committed to the job.

It was a pleasant space trip back to Venezeli. Duandarin had used the three days to study his materials and Journal. Once back in Venezeli, Duandarin was shown to his new accommodation in Ipa. The Collective headed back to Fraz County.

The Collective took part in the Laying Down ceremony in the Herratta cavern. It was a beautiful ceremony that lasted around five days. Enchantments were made. Strong binds, which required a lot of magical prowess, were set in the cavern walls. In two days' time, The Collective would be heading back to Ipa for the Koli Ceremony. The Judges had moved to Ipa that week. Those who had been found first took time to walk around Ipa and get to know Ozro. Those who were found later stayed in their new homes in the Judges' quarter, brushing up on all the monthly paperwork and Journals they had to read. Duandarin was told to just read what he could. The Judges would have a further twelve months to learn everything they had to know.

After the Laying Down ceremony, The Collective headed to the far Easy Fraz coastline for two days to celebrate the wedding of Carmen De La Luz and Shine Cedar. It was a beautiful ceremony. Carmen was dressed in a red wedding dress made by her mother. Shine was in a green and white gown she had made herself. The first day was full of preparations and relaxation. The Collective worked hard to get everything ready. On the second day, the guests arrived. All eleven Judges were invited to the wedding. Meradin Zykló and Danny Dove were asked to be witnesses. Jakolyn Tempest accompanied Luther as his plus one. It was an enjoyable way for the Judges to meet each other, informally, before their inauguration ceremony in Ipa in two days' time.

Six massively long rectangular tables were set in the heart of the woodlands, by the beach. At them, sat Tomms Day, Ignacius Prime, Lara Trinkett, Bird Night, Zoop Harvey, Shamus Montgomery, Meradin Zykló, Romins Perpula-Dawn, Jakolyn Tempest, Danny Dove, Duandarin Krespos, The Collective, friends from the Shamanic Community, Cressida, Hispanica, Carmen's mother and Christian Travis, who came as Serenity's plus one. All the Judges, except Tomms who was from Fraz County, couldn't believe how much the air smelled of sweet pine trees and cedarwood – it was a heady and wonderful breath of fresh air.

At the ceremony, Carmen presented Shine with one of her mother's handkerchiefs.

"I'd like you to have it. It's important to me, and so are you."

Shine took the handkerchief, folded it, and placed it inside the top of her dress.

"I'll always keep it on my person, forever and ever." They eat and drank and danced until the early hours. Carmen noticed Tomms and Shamus sharing a slow dance under the stars. Shine notices that Meradin and Duandarin had been inseparable since the ceremony and were sitting on two whiskey barrels in the corner of the manufactured forest dance floor. They hadn't stopped talking all evening.

"Are these guys having an innocent dance, or could we be responsible for some Supreme Court hook ups?" said Carmen, as she danced with her bride.

"They look lovely together," replied Shine, "Meradin and Duandarin seem to have hit it off too. There's nothing in the rule book that says they can't couple up." smiled Shine, "They have a job to do, and there's no reason why this would stop them. We've selected them for their integrity and maturity to act in accordance to what's right for Venezeli. To deny them romantic feelings for another is to deny their Venezelian flesh, blood, heart and soul."

"Exactly," said Carmen, "we chose these people because we believe they can do their job, make rational decisions and exist in a beautiful relationship, without it hazing their judgement."

"I'd argue it's absolutely do-able." said Shine.

"I'd second that judgement." said Carmen with a laugh, giving her bride a tender kiss.

CHAPTER TWENTY-TWO
The Koli Ceremony

"The Journals say times will get worse before they get better." said a holographic image of Jimus Krakovia. "Factions will arise. This period of reflection and appreciation will end, such are our natures. Those with a strong will and kind heart will stay the course. Weaker members of our society will be tempted by the darkness and find themselves consumed by it once again."

The Collective were sitting on benches in a semi-constructed court room. They were encased in just two metres of wall at the moment. There were no ceilings or major features yet. On the temporary stage, erected in front of them, stood the eleven Judges in their ceremonial gowns. Venezelian officials from Ipa were dotted around the room with clip boards and recording devices. This was a special moment in Venezelian history. Behind The Collective sat Cressida and other helpers from Fraz County. These helpers had organised the deployment of information, alongside Ipa officials, for the eleven Judges.

The surup was high in the sky and a warm and welcomed breeze swirled its way into the barely outlined court room.

Some of the newly appointed officials from MEW5, CERN and the dream academy were assembled outside to congratulate the Judges after the ceremony.

Jimus Krakovia's hologram continued its speech. "Tensions will rise again, competition will thrive, a Revolution will be born. Things will come to a spectacular climax somewhere down the line. Remember, nothing is set in stone. This prophecy is a guide. Study your Journals of what is, read the signs, keep the peace and all of this will help you make the best decisions to play the game."

Tremendos was watching Danny Dove. He had the shakes. She threw him a smile. He smiled back and the shakes seemed to diminish slightly.

"Judges, you will have the last word on all matters. Please value this honour. We know you won't abuse it. We know you won't be bought or swayed. We know you will act with valour and compassion and love – it's why you were chosen. Reason to the best of your will."

Luther glances lovingly at Jakolyn, whom, he could tell, was desperately trying to hold back her tears. He had tissues in his pocket, ready, for after the ceremony. He was so proud of her. He was proud of all the Judges and of The Collective. Luther planned to propose to Jakolyn at their celebratory meal in Ipa that evening.

"Shamans and Visionary," continued Jimus, "take pride in your Pilgrimage. Your leader has chosen well, and so have you."

Cressida stroked Hispanica's long hair. She was very proud of The Collective. Cressida felt happy that Hispanica had such a decent Supreme Court in place to watch over her, and the next generation. A Supreme Court that would always protect her rights and her freedoms.

"As we face good years and bad," said Jimus, "easy and tough, what matters isn't whether we can stop the bad from coming. It's about doing our best now, to prevent those hard times from becoming too difficult to navigate through in the first place. This takes an ongoing commitment. This takes years of love and investment, not a desperate flush attempt at the eleventh hour. Let us learn from our past mistakes as a species – recognise the important things in our society. So many planets repeat the same mistakes. This is our biggest takeaway from The Awakening – let us not repeat the negative forces. Let us not put in power those who would harm us and just better their own situation. This is unjust, not right. Not in any cosmos or any universe. Let us value our values and protect our people always - not just when crisis hits."

To his own surprise, Colonius was welling up. Serenity passed him a tissue.

"When the tough times come again, and they will, there will be elements that are out with our control. What will matter is how we decide to deal with it. You must be united in your judgements and proactive in your commitment to help. Where there is disagreement, where issues cannot be resolved, it goes to the Supreme Court and a democratic vote."

Cressida left the bench and made her way to the stage. The Judges took each other's hands. Cressida picked up a small wooden bowl with some thick red liquid inside. It had a waxy consistency and smelled of Frankincense.

Cressida started to walk down the line of Judges. She placed three lines on the heads of the Judges. These represented the three fingers Jimus Krakovia from Freyal extended to Sister Pretya from Naboxulus during their moment of First Contact.

They planned to do a fresco inside the Supreme Court's dome room to commemorate it.

As Cressida walked down the line, she initiated a chant.

"Aumm-ah-neah. Aumm-ah-neah." Cressida would say it twice, and each Judge would repeat it back twice.

And so, it was done.

All eleven judges were inaugurated. Everybody bustled outside the construction site of the Supreme Court.

Colonius stopped in his tracks. His mother and father were standing next to a group of Ipa officials. They had come to celebrate their son's achievement and the appointment of the new Judges. Colonius walked over to them.

"What are you doing here?"

"We got your letter, son." replied Francis Bramblebush Jnr.

"But I didn't hear back from you. I thought you were…disappointed."

"We were shocked, at first," said his mother, "but we are so proud of you."

"You are?" asked Colonius, in disbelief.

"We knew your letter came from the heart. We owe you an apology, in person. We didn't know you felt that way, and for all those years." Margaret Bramblebush took her son's hands.

"We're sorry, son."

"We really are," said Francis, "and we are proud of you. You took control of your life long ago. We didn't see it that way at the time. We were disappointed that you didn't choose the path we had in mind for you. But as you said in your letter, sometimes someone must break the chain. Your mother and I lived in the shadow of our parents' expectations of us, and we didn't even know it. That isn't love. Giving your child the freedom and encouragement to follow their own path – that is love."

"And good parenting." added Margaret. She hugged Colonius. "It is safe, this Shamanism thing?

"Yes, mother." Colonius laughed, but he had tears in his eyes.

Colonius pulled his father in for a group hug. He held them tighter than he'd ever done before.

"I really wanted to visit you, when we were in Ozro."

"Well you can now, and anytime you want to. And we'll come and visit you, in Fraz County. Your mother's always wanted to smell the air there too."

Colonius laughed. "Want to join us for the celebratory meal?"

"We'd love to." said Francis.

***

The Morning Before The Koli Ceremony

Luther had around two hours before he was due at the Supreme Court site. His mother's ring was in his breast pocket. He was on his way to a Watch-And-Wait ring vendor. He planned to get the ring sized up for Jakolyn.

The Grassmarket was bustling. Luther meandered his way through the crowds. There was a slight morning mist over the busy jade cobbled streets ahead of him. Someone bumped into him. Luther was worried that he has just accidentally clipped said person with his broad frame. He was sure they had just banged their forehead into his shoulders by mistake. It was a woman.

"I'm so sorry Miss, are you ok?" he asked.

The woman turned, disorientated at first, then looked up.

"Luther?"

Luther looked down – it was Leeying Crown.

"Leeying. How are you?" Luther felt a little sick. This was the last person he was expecting to see this morning.

"I'm great, I mean, I'm fine." she pulled Luther by the jacket sleeve, moving him out of the way of the swaying bodies on the Grassmarket street. They were standing in-between a Glup Jock stand and a tomaten vendor.

The Grassmarket continued its fast flow. For Leeying, everything slowed down.

"You made it to Ipa."

"It's the ceremony today."

"Oh yes," replied Leeying, "of course."

"How are things for you?"

"Well I made it into the educational consultancy world."

"That's great Leeying! That's what you always wanted. And your husband?"

"Well... we never made it that far. It didn't work out. I'm on my own again."

"I'm sorry to hear it didn't work out. What's meant to be, is meant to be though, right?"

"Right! Listen, do you have time, I mean, do you want to go for a coffee?"

"I'm sorry," said Luther, "it's not the right time."

"How about later? Or on another day? You can tell me all about your Pilgrimage, your life in Fraz County." enquired Leeying.

"Actually, I'm moving to Ipa, to the Judges' quarters."

"Wow! That's great, we should definitely meet up."

"I'm sorry Leeying. It's been lovely to bump into you like this, but I don't think that coffee is going to happen. A lot of time has passed and, well, I've met someone."

"Oh…I see."

Luther realised, all at once, that what he had felt for Leeying was never true love. It was lust. It was infatuation. He had been in love with the idea of being in love. Back then, he would have done anything for her, despite the ways in which she hurt him. She rejected him. She never tried contacting him when she moved to Ipa, yet he pined for her. That scared him. His mind went back to the waters at Shark Bay. Love isn't blind. True love sees right into the heart of you, and it never lets you go.

"You know, our paths probably won't cross again, but that doesn't mean that you weren't an important part of my life. Everyone is important, everyone teaches you something. You will find your soul mate, Leeying. Just be open to it."

"I'm glad you found someone, Luther."

"It's funny," said Luther, "we thought this Pilgrimage was about finding the Supreme Court Judges. It was so much more than that. We found ourselves again." Luther placed a hand on Leeying's shoulder. "When you left for Ipa, you were listening to the beat of your own drum. You followed it. Never lose that, Leeying. It is one of the greatest things we can ever learn about ourselves. To forget the crowd and carry on into the unknown, guided only by an instinct. It takes courage."

Leeying smiled.

"Take care, Leeying. I truly wish you all the best."

"Good-bye, Luther." Luther smiled and said goodbye. He disappeared into the crowd once more.

Arriving at the Watch-and-Wait, he handed over the ring with a beaming smile. He turned to look out at the busy streets of Ipa, its locals going about their day. Luther believed it now, more than ever. There were new days ahead, for everyone – and they would be filled with opportunities for good.

THE END

ABOUT THE AUTHOR

Adriana Polito lives in Scotland with her husband, Tom.

Six Shamans And A Visionary is her first novella.
It is her second book, and the prequel to her debut novel,
The World Within.

Adriana enjoys dreaming, learning about the human brain and spending time with her family.

During the pandemic, she tried learning to bake.
She still cannot bake.

Adriana is a lover of film. When she writes, she visualizes her stories frame by frame. Like most storytellers, she would love to see her books on the big screen one day.